TAUNTING CALLUM

A BIG SKY ROYAL NOVEL

KRISTEN PROBY

AMPERSAND PUBLISHING, INC.

Taunting Callum
A Big Sky Novel
By
Kristen Proby

TAUNTING CALLUM

A Big Sky Royal Novel

Kristen Proby

Copyright © 2020 by Kristen Proby

All Rights Reserved. This book may not be reproduced, scanned, or distributed in any printed or electronic form without permission from the author. Please do not participate in or encourage piracy of copyrighted materials in violation of the author's rights. All characters and storylines are the property of the author and your support and respect are appreciated. The characters and events portrayed in this book are fictitious. Any similarity to real persons, living or dead, is coincidental and not intended by the author.

Cover Design: By Hang Le

Paperback ISBN: 978-1-63350-070-9

Published by Ampersand Publishing, Inc.

GLOSSARY

Who's who in Cunningham Falls...

Please know this may contain spoilers for anyone new to the series. The books each couple stars in is noted next to their description.

The King Family:

Jeff and Nancy King – Retired owners of the Lazy K Ranch. Parents of Josh and Zack King.

Josh King – Partner of Lazy K Ranch. Married to Cara Donovan. {Loving Cara}

Zack King – Partner of Lazy K Ranch. Married to Jillian Sullivan (Jillian is the sister of Ty Sullivan). Parents to Seth, Miles and Sarah. {Falling for Jillian}

Doug and Susan King – Doug is Jeff's brother. They live mostly in Arizona, but come to Montana in the summer. Parents of Noah and Grayson.

Noah King – Owner of Wild Wings Bird Sanctuary. Married to Fallon McCarthy, a yoga instructor and owner of Asana Yoga Studio. {Soaring With Fallon}

Grayson King – Ski Instructor on Whitetail Ski Resort. Married to Autumn O'Dea, a Pop music sensation. {Hold On, A Crossover Novella by Samantha Young}

The Sullivan Family:

Ty Sullivan – Attorney. Brother of Jillian. Married to Lauren Cunningham, a bestselling author, whose great grandfather first settled Cunningham Falls. Parents to Layla. {Seducing Lauren}

The Hull Family:

Brad Hull – Chief of Police. Married to Hannah Malone, an OB/GYN. {Charming Hannah}

Jenna Hull – Owner of Snow Wolf Lodge. Married to actor and superstar, Christian Wolfe. {Kissing Jenna}

Max Hull – Self-made billionaire. Married to Willa Monroe (Sister to Jesse Anderson), owner of Dress It Up. Parents to Alex Monroe. {Waiting for Willa}

The Henderson Family:

Brooke Henderson – Owner of Brooke's Blooms. Married to Brody Chabot, architect. {Tempting Brooke, a 1001 Dark Nights Novella}

Maisey Henderson – Owner of Cake Nation. Married to Tucker McCloud, pro football player. {Nothing Without You, A Crossover Novella by Monica Murphy}

The Royal Family:

Prince Sebastian Wakefield – The Duke of Somerset. Married to Nina Wolfe (sister to Christian). {Enchanting Sebastian}

Prince Frederick Wakefield – Brother to Sebastian. Married to Catherine. No book belongs to this couple, as they are already married when introduced.

Prince Callum – Brother to Sebastian. Married to Aspen Calhoun, the new owner of Drips & Sips.

Princess Eleanor Wakefield – Sister to Sebastian. Married to Liam Cunningham. {Enticing Liam}

Jacob Baxter – Sebastian's best friend. Owner of Whitetail Mountain, along with several local businesses, including the restaurant Ciao. Married to Grace Douglas.

Liam Cunningham – Head of Montana security, and personal bodyguard to Sebastian. Cousin to Lauren Cunningham. Married to Ellie Wakefield. {Enticing Liam}

Nick Ferguson – Personal bodyguard to Nina Wolfe.

Miscellaneous and important characters:

Jesse Anderson - Former Navy deep-sea diver. Married to Tara Hunter. {Worth Fighting For, A Crossover Collection Novella by Laura Kaye}

Joslyn Meyers – Pop star. Married to Kynan McGrath. {Wicked Force, A Crossover Collection Novella by Sawyer Bennett}

Dr. Drake Merritt – Surgeon. Married to Abigail Darwin. Both characters are best friends of Hannah Malone. {Crazy Imperfect Love, A Crossover Collection Novella by K. L. Grayson}

Penelope (Penny) – Former teacher. Married to Trevor Wood, Drummer for the rock band, Adrenaline. {All

Stars Fall, A Crossover Collection Novella by Rachel Van Dyken}

Sam Waters – Firefighter, Liam Cunningham's best friend.

PROLOGUE

~ASPEN~

Two Years Ago

Maybe taking goodies over to the royal family this morning was a stupid move. I mean, I got accosted by security for my efforts and was completely embarrassed. What was I thinking? They're *royalty*. They don't need my pastries to make them feel better. They probably have people to make baked goods for them.

But they just went through a horrible scare, with search and rescue being called in and everything, and I know how that feels. Intimately. Luckily for them, their outcome was very different from mine, but I know how exhausting it is. And the last thing you want to think about the next day is food.

And damn it, Cunningham Falls is a small community. A tight-knit one. And we take care of each other here. At least, that's what I've learned in the short time I've been here. And I like it.

So, I took them a basket full of freshly baked pastries and plenty of coffee to get them all through the morning. Once I got past the guys in suits, I was in and out of there. No need to dawdle and make it even more embarrassing than it already was.

I didn't anticipate one of the prince's running after me to introduce himself.

I also didn't figure he'd be hotter in person than he is on TV and in magazines, but holy Christ on a cracker, Callum is sexier than sin. And he *asked me to dinner.*

I shake my head as I pull the portafilter out of the espresso machine and get to work giving it a good cleaning.

The offer was flattering. And more than surprising. But come on, he's a freaking *prince.* And I'm a small-town girl with enough emotional baggage to fill the cargo hold of a cruise ship.

There's no future in that.

Not that he insinuated in any way, shape, or form that he wanted a *future.* But still.

I'm totally overthinking this.

Maybe he was just being kind and grateful because I brought food.

I nod and move on to emptying a dishwasher full of coffee mugs.

Yes, that's it. He was being nice.

And I've been overthinking it all day. I mixed up people's drinks, forgot one altogether, and my head has been in the clouds.

As the new owner of Drips & Sips in Cunningham Falls, Montana, I'm a professional. I need to remember what my priorities are and keep my mind on the task at hand.

And that is running this amazing business, not wondering about the flirtations of a member of the royal family.

"Get it together, Aspen," I mutter just as the bell on the door dings behind me, signaling that someone is walking in. "Sorry, we're closed for the day."

I turn and stop short.

Callum Wakefield, *Prince* Callum Wakefield, is standing in my café.

"Yes, I was banking on that," he says with a wink and flips the lock on the door before turning back to me. "How was your day?"

"Uh, busy," I reply and frown in confusion at the tall, sexy man as he walks closer. He's in jeans and a green, short-sleeve, button-down shirt. He's tanned, and his square jawline has the slightest hint of scruff.

His brown eyes, full of humor and mischief, are on me as I soak him in.

"What can I do for you?" I ask and set my wet rag

aside. I want to fiddle with my hair—I know I look horrible after a long day of work—but I don't.

"You can go to dinner with me," he says with a half-smile.

I laugh. I can't help myself. Am I being punked? Since when does royalty ask *Aspen Calhoun* out on a date?

"Is something about that funny?" he asks.

"Hilarious," I confirm. "What can I really do for you? I just cleaned the espresso machine, but I can make you something if you like."

"I believe I'm speaking English," he says and leans on my counter. "I'd like to have dinner with you."

I narrow my eyes. "No, thank you."

He tilts his head to the side. "Drinks?"

"I'd rather not."

"I'll buy you some coffee, then."

I laugh again. "I get all the coffee I want for free."

He nods, watching me with those intense brown eyes. "Well, why don't I just hang out here while you close up?"

"Where's your security?" I ask as I turn and continue putting mugs away. "Don't you go everywhere with them in tow?"

"Waiting outside," he replies, walking up beside me. "Why are you here alone?"

"Because I like being alone," I reply honestly. "There's no need to pay staff to stay late. Besides, I kind of like to clean. It allows me to think."

He doesn't say anything. He also doesn't make a move to leave.

So, I reach into a bucket and retrieve another rag, wring it out, and pass it to him.

"Here. If you're going to hang out, you can make yourself useful."

He raises a brow, but he takes the rag from me.

"What would you like me to do with this?"

"Wipe off tables," I reply, gesturing toward the back of the café. "Just give them a little pass over with the rag."

"Yes, ma'am."

He immediately turns away and gets to work, surprising the hell out of me. I expected him to smirk and pass the rag back.

He's a prince.

And he's cleaning tables in my café.

If it weren't so absurd, it would be adorable.

Maybe I hit my head earlier today, and this is all just a funny dream. I'll have to call my friend Natasha later and tell her all about it. She'll get a kick out of it.

But when I turn around and find Callum standing there, watching me, it feels very real.

"You're not a dream, are you?"

His lips tip up in an arrogant smile. "Well, in what context are you referring?"

Why is his accent so damn sexy? I mean, he looks like *that*, and he sounds sexy, as well? Inconceivable.

"This is the most bizarre conversation I've ever had.

And trust me when I say I've had some crazy encounters. What are you doing here?"

"I told you," he says, setting the rag on the counter and walking around to me once more. "I want to take you to dinner. Or *somewhere*. I'd like to get to know you better, Aspen."

I lick my lips. He's so close now, I can feel the heat of him. He would scramble the brains of any warm-blooded woman.

But I haven't flirted with a man in years. And I certainly haven't entertained the idea of dating one. Or, better yet, having sex with one.

But with Callum standing mere feet away, that's precisely what I'm thinking.

"You surprise me," I admit in a soft voice.

"How's that?"

"You cleaned those tables without batting an eye."

"I've cleaned far worse, I can assure you."

I tilt my head, watching him. I can see his pulse in his neck.

"You're a prince."

He narrows his eyes and moves in closer, not touching me but certainly crowding. He smells like mint and sunshine.

"I'm just a man, Aspen." His lips graze my cheek. "A man very taken with you, I might add."

I swallow hard. Holy shit. My breathing comes harder, and an ache sets up shop in my very core.

I want him.

I don't think I've ever been so attracted to a man before. Not even Greg. No one.

And if I ponder that for too long, the guilt will likely set in.

Instead, I turn my head and brush my nose over his jawline.

I want him to *touch me.* I want to feel things that have been missing from my life for *years.*

Suddenly, I want it with this perfect stranger.

"Aspen," he whispers.

"Yes."

"Tell me you don't feel this."

I swallow again. "I can't."

He growls as he plunges his hands into my hair and closes his lips over mine in the kiss of the century. His moves are smooth and sure. Assertive.

That's what Callum is: confident.

But before the kiss goes any further, he backs up and stares down at me with intense brown eyes.

"I can't do what I want to you here. All of bloody Montana could look through those windows, and I won't have you caught in a scandal."

"Office," I reply immediately. With his hand in mine, I lead him through to the back of the café and my personal space there. It's not fancy, but it's private.

"Brilliant," he says as he shuts the door behind him. Once I've pulled the blinds on the window, he comes right for me. He frames my face with his hands as he kisses me again, deeper and harder than before. We're a tangle of material and limbs as we hurry out of our clothes. Suddenly, he boosts me up onto my desk.

And I can't stop staring at his bare arm.

It's covered in ink from his shoulder to his mid-forearm. Right where the rolled-up sleeve of his dress shirt would end.

"You have tattoos," I say.

"Several," he agrees and smiles just before he rips a condom wrapper open with his teeth. Where he got it, I have no idea, but I'm damn grateful he has it. And then he's moving over me, and inside me, as if he'll die if he doesn't fuck me *right now*.

I cry out, but not in fear or pain. No, this might be the best sex of my life, and I can't get enough.

"So fucking beautiful," he murmurs against my breast before tugging my nipple into his mouth, sending me over into an orgasm that would make the gods weep in gratitude. "That's it, love. Again."

I shake my head, but I'll be damned if I don't fall over that edge again, and then once more when he presses the pad of his thumb against my clit.

I'm a shaking, gasping mess when Callum buries his face in my neck and succumbs to his climax.

∼

One Year Later

. . .

It's been a hell of a day, and I'm ready to close up shop and go home, pour a glass of wine, and stare at the mountains from my back deck for the rest of the evening.

Owning a business is rewarding and wonderful. It also kicks my ass on the daily.

I'm thinking of my back deck view when the bell over the door sounds. I glance up to see my friend, Princess Ellie, walk in with her security, along with her brother, Callum and his security detail.

Holy shit, Callum's in town.

I haven't seen him since that day here in my café. I've never told a soul about what happened—even Ellie. Since she's been living in Cunningham Falls this summer, she and I have become good friends. But she doesn't need to know that I had a one-night stand with her brother.

Or, more specifically, a single, late afternoon stand.

I mean, it was just incredible, earth-shattering sex. The kind that sticks with a girl for the rest of her life, no matter what happens after the fact. And I'm content keeping it for myself.

It's a happy memory.

After losing my husband and daughter so many years ago, a memory that makes me smile is exactly what I need.

"Hey, Aspen," Ellie says with a big grin. "I believe you've met my brother, Callum."

I'm just about to agree when he frowns and shakes his head. "No, I don't believe we have."

I blink rapidly. *Are you fucking kidding me?*

Just like that, my happy memory pops like a balloon.

He was the best sex of my life. The *only* sex I've had since my husband died, and *he doesn't remember it?*

The next few minutes are a haze as Ellie and Callum place their orders and sit at one of the nearby tables. Callum faces my way, watching me work.

He *forgot* me.

I shake my head as I pour milk into a carafe.

He forgot.

Sure, it was a year ago, but he just walked into my café, into the place where he was *inside* me, and he…forgot.

I don't want it to hurt. I really, really don't.

But it does. It's a knife in the back, and I feel like I'm going to throw up. The chemistry was off the charts. The sex was incredible.

Or so I thought.

But I guess, according to Callum, the encounter was utterly forgettable.

And that makes me feel cheap and, frankly, like garbage. I was discarded plenty as a kid. It hurts just as bad as an adult.

I deliver their order, and the asshole has the fucking audacity to ask me out to dinner.

The answer to that is a *hell no.*

My friend Willa comes in with her son, Alex, which is a nice distraction. Maybe Ellie and Callum will just take their stuff and go.

But after Willa leaves, I realize I'm not so lucky.

Callum approaches the counter, and I square my shoulders.

"Aspen," Callum begins. "I owe you a big apology. I just got off the plane after being up for thirty hours, and—"

I hold up my hand, and he closes his mouth.

"Is there something else you need?" My hands are shaking, so I link them behind my back and hope he doesn't notice. I want to throw up. I want to cry.

But I won't do any of that, not in front of him.

"Yes, to bloody apologize," he says, but I shake my head. "I didn't mean to hurt your feelings."

"Let's get something straight," I reply immediately, feeling the blood rushing to my cheeks in anger. "You didn't hurt me. It takes a hell of a lot more than an egotistical, full-of-himself prince to hurt me. Besides, you don't know me, remember? What do you care?"

"Well, I—"

"That was a rhetorical question," I add. "Now, if there's nothing more I can do for you, I'm closing early today."

"We're leaving," Ellie says, pulling on Callum's arm as she looks back at me in apology. "Thank you, Aspen. Let's get together soon, okay?"

I smile at my friend. "I'd love that, Ellie. I'll text you soon."

"Lovely." She pushes Callum toward the door. "Let's go."

Once they're gone, I rush to the door and lock it. When I'm alone in my office, I let the tears come.

The son of a bitch *forgot me.* I didn't expect him to fall over himself to see me or say hello. But to completely forget? It's absolutely unforgivable.

I wipe my cheeks and resolve not to shed another tear for Callum Wakefield.

CHAPTER 1

~ASPEN~

Present Day

"I hate today," I mutter as I climb out of my car in front of Brooke's Blooms and walk inside the beautiful floral shop. It's late summer, and the fragrance that assaults my nostrils is glorious. This used to be my favorite time of year.

Used to be.

"Hey, Aspen," Brooke says with a wide smile. She's a pretty, petite woman with dark hair and an artistic eye for flowers. She never ceases to amaze me. I couldn't put a bouquet together to save my life. And, thankfully, I don't have to. Because I have Brooke.

"Good morning," I reply. "I'm here to pick up the wreaths."

"Of course. I'll grab them from the cooler."

She steps into the walk-in refrigerator. A few moments later, she comes back holding two wreaths, each about two feet in diameter, before setting them on the countertop.

"Beautiful," I whisper and gently tickle the petals of a sunflower with my fingertips. "You did a wonderful job, Brooke."

"I'm glad you like them," she says. "Are these for your front door? Or for Drips & Sips?"

I shake my head but offer her a small smile. "No, they're just something pretty to remember something I lost. Thanks again. You outdid yourself."

I square the tab with her and leave the shop, a wreath in each hand as I walk back out to my car.

The drive to the little state park at the edge of Whitetail Lake doesn't take long. It's a beautiful late September morning. The sun is up, the birds chirping.

And I'm here to remember my dead husband and daughter.

I take the wreaths from the car and walk down to the shoreline. I'm alone down here, which I counted on. I don't need anyone witnessing my grief. I'm a loner, an introvert at heart, and aside from a few very close friends, this isn't something I plan to share with anyone. Especially strangers.

I squat next to the water and pick up Greg's wreath first. I chose red peonies and lots of greens for his wreath. The peonies were in my wedding bouquet, and the greens are because Greg enjoyed being out in the wilderness more than almost anything. He said it's where his heart was on fire.

And it killed him.

It killed both of them.

I was angry for a long time, but I can look back with bittersweet fondness now. I loved my husband with a passion. He was my match in every way. Had been with me since high school when I bounced from foster home to foster home.

When we got pregnant at sixteen, he didn't leave me. He didn't bail. He stuck right by me. Despite being painfully young and completely out of our element, we welcomed Emma into the world and did the best we could.

He worked two jobs. And with a ton of hard work and grit, we beat the odds. We had a loving marriage, a healthy, happy child, and a fantastic life.

I kiss one of the flowers, set the wreath on the water, and give it a push and watch as it travels over the calm surface.

"Rest easy, Greg," I whisper and then look down at the second wreath.

This one is still a sucker punch to the gut.

My perfect baby girl was the light of my life. Her little laugh could make the sunshine seem dim. She had my red hair and her dad's love of nature. The dirtier she got, the better. I fought a never-ending battle trying to keep her clean.

When Greg wanted to go camping one last time that summer, and I had to work, Emma was thrilled at the idea of spending two whole days with her daddy in the woods. I stayed back, working the shifts at the restaurant that I couldn't get out of. But secretly, I wasn't upset. Camping wasn't really my thing.

It was theirs.

I brush my fingers over the sunflowers and sniff as tears fill my eyes. These flowers remind me of Emma, her bright smile and happy personality.

She was only seven when she was taken away from me.

She'd be a teenager this year.

I kiss the sunflower lightly. "Sweet dreams, baby girl."

And then I push the wreath onto the water and watch it glide out to sit next to Greg's, as if the energies of the universe pull them together.

They always were two peas in a pod.

I sit for a while on the shoreline and watch the flowers floating on the water until they drift out of sight.

And then I sit for a little longer.

Today is the one day every year that I let myself be sad, remember, and cry.

I hear a car door slam behind me. That's my cue to leave.

I stand and walk back to my vehicle, but rather than

go immediately home, I drive downtown and park in front of Asana Yoga Studio.

I need to breathe and stretch and re-center myself.

"I thought you said you wouldn't be here," the studio owner says as I walk inside.

"I changed my mind," I tell Fallon with a shrug. "I didn't bring the right clothes, but I don't care. Can I borrow a mat?"

"You can borrow anything you want," she says and then lays her hand on my shoulder. "Are you okay, friend?"

"I will be." I offer her a brave smile, and then I'm rescued as other clients walk in for class. I don't want to answer any more questions.

I roll out a mat. Before long, Fallon is taking us through meditation, breathing, and guiding our poses.

By the time the hour is up, I feel much calmer. More at peace.

Well, as peaceful as I can be on this day, anyway.

And as I leave the studio and take a deep breath of fresh air, I know that coming here today was the right choice. If not, I'd just be at home, moping. And that's not healthy.

I can't go into work for the rest of the day. I promised to take the day off. I'd just be distracted anyway.

So, I head for my little house at the edge of town. I love the view of the mountains from my back deck. Honestly, the entire house suits me.

It's a little quirky. Sometimes irritable. Mostly endearing.

I pull into the driveway and feel my eyebrows climb at the sight of my two best friends, Monica and Natasha, sitting on my front porch.

"There you are," Monica says as I walk toward them. "I thought you'd be home an hour ago."

"I decided to go to yoga," I reply and eye the bags they're holding. "What's up?"

"Well, we know what today is," Natasha says as she pushes her dark hair behind her ear. These two are the *only* ones in Cunningham Falls who know. "And we decided that you're not going to spend it by yourself."

"You decided?"

"Yep. Don't try to give us attitude, either," Monica adds. "You're stuck with us."

"Unlock the door," Natasha instructs me, pointing to the keyholes.

"Bossy, aren't you?" I climb the steps and unlock the deadbolt, then step inside and lead them both through the living space to the kitchen, where I open the fridge and reach for a pitcher of filtered water. "Want some?"

"We have better beverages than that," Monica says. "Natasha's making her famous 'ritas."

I check the time. "It's not even eleven in the morning."

"It's five o'clock somewhere," Natasha says with a shrug and starts unpacking tequila, limes, and salt from one of the bags. "Look, when it's the anniversary of your husband's and daughter's deaths, you get a pass on what time of day is socially acceptable to day drink."

"We also brought guac and pico and queso," Monica says.

"The trifecta of corn chip goodness," I say and smile at my friends. "I thought I wanted to be alone today, but I think you're right. This is much better."

"Of course, we're right," Monica says. "Duh."

"I wish Ellie was here," Natasha says. "She's so fun. Oh, but maybe you don't want her to know."

"Ellie's my friend, and I trust her," I say with a sigh and reach for a tortilla chip, load it up with guacamole, and shove it into my mouth whole. "Eventually, I'll tell her. Someday. Although, given she's royalty, she probably already knows. I'm sure the minute we started spending time together, they did a deep-dive into my past."

"You're probably right. She's coming to town," Natasha adds. "I heard from her the other day. She and Liam, and Sebastian and Nina are coming to spend a few weeks and enjoy the rest of summer."

"It's good timing," Monica says. "We're having an awesome late summer. The weather will be perfect."

I nod and continue shoveling chips into my mouth. I had no idea I was so hungry.

"She gets here Friday," I say and take a sip of the margarita that Natasha just passed me. "Oh shit, that's strong."

"You're welcome," Natasha says with a grin. "We'll

have to see if she wants to do girls' night Saturday. We haven't seen her in a few months."

"I haven't seen her since her wedding," I reply and try to block that night out of my mind. It's not that the wedding wasn't absolutely spectacular. It was the best one I've ever been to.

But Callum danced with me at the reception.

I hate that guy.

Thankfully, I haven't seen the prince since the wedding either. I don't need that mistake thrown in my face at every turn.

Even Natasha and Monica don't know that I had the best sex of my life with Ellie's brother. Or that he promptly forgot all about it.

How humiliating.

What a jerk.

"Right?"

I glance up. "Huh?"

Monica smiles. "I said this might be the best guac I've made."

"I'm shoveling it in, aren't I?"

She nods smugly. "Indeed, you are."

"You know," Natasha says as we load everything into our arms and take it onto the deck, "we should have mid-morning margaritas more often."

"I don't think that would go over well with my clients," Monica says with a laugh. "Although, we might get some interesting haircuts out of it."

Monica owns The Style Studio, the hair and nail

salon downtown next to Asana Yoga. She does hair, and Natasha does nails. There's also a massage therapist, an eyelash specialist, and two other hairstylists.

It's one of my favorite places in town.

"Wait." I frown at both of my friends. "Did you guys take today off to be here?"

"Cleared our books," Monica confirms. "And I told Rich that I'd be gone all day, but that he could reach me on my cell if he needs me."

I feel the tears threaten again.

"You guys didn't have to do that."

"We're your family," Natasha says as she leans over and covers my hand with hers. "And it's a tough day. So, of course, there's nowhere else we'd be, Aspen."

"Damn it, I hate crying." I brush a tear from my cheek. "I was doing so well today, too."

"Do you want to talk about it?" Monica asks quietly. "You've never told us *how*, just that it happened."

"No." I swallow hard. Reliving that weekend is never something I want to do. "No, I don't want to talk about it."

"More guac?" Natasha asks, offering me the bowl.

"Yes, that's perfect. And more margaritas."

"That we can do."

"I THOUGHT TOURIST SEASON WAS OVER," Gretchen, my assistant manager, says Friday afternoon as we hustle through the tail-end of the lunch crowd.

Wendy and Kelli, my morning workers, both left an hour ago. Gretchen and I are usually fine without help in the afternoons.

But the crowds gave us a run for our money today. I'll never be sorry for the extra business, though. And now that most of the tables are empty, and it's calmed down, I'm grateful.

"Maybe the weather lured in more tourists for the weekend?" I ask and eye the display case. "Either way, we're out of almost everything. I'll never complain about that."

"No, it's fantastic," Gretchen says as she replaces the vanilla syrup. "Those new huckleberry chutney turkey sandwiches are divine. They flew out of here."

"I like trying new things. And when the customers go crazy for them, even better."

Gretchen smiles, and her eyes light up when someone approaches the counter. "Hey there, Chief."

I turn to find our police chief, Brad Hull, standing at the counter.

"Do you need your usual afternoon shot of caffeine?" I ask with a smile.

"Please," he replies. "How's business?"

"Busier than expected," I admit as I pour two percent into a carafe and flip on the hot air to froth the milk. "Is something special happening this weekend in town?"

"Just excellent late summer weather," he says. "The lake will be loaded with boats, and the trails with hikers this weekend. But the cooler weather is supposed to move in next week."

"So, I'll take the business while I can get it," I say and pass him the cup of coffee. "It's on the house. Be safe this weekend."

"Appreciate it," he says and takes a sip. "Best coffee in town."

"Damn right, it is."

He winks and then walks out of the café. I turn to find Gretchen wistfully watching Brad walk away.

"He's a married man," I remind her. "Might want to ogle someone single."

"I know." She sighs dramatically. "And I like Hannah. But it's a damn shame."

"It's a shame that he's happily married?"

"That he's not happily married to me," Gretchen says.

"Weren't you infatuated with some firefighter last week?"

She grins. "Yeah. I think I have a thing for men in uniform."

"I mean, who doesn't?" I ask and laugh with Gretchen as she pulls her apron off and rolls it up to put in her locker.

"Everything's clean, restocked, and the place is finally empty."

"Go enjoy the rest of the day," I say and wave her off. "If any stragglers come in, I can handle it."

"Thanks, boss." She hurries back to stow her apron, retrieve her purse and keys, and then she's out the door—most likely to look for a man for the weekend.

I like Gretchen. She has an excellent work ethic, and I can depend on her to be here on time, and to work her whole shift. But she's also ridiculously boy-crazy.

And she's twenty-six.

I shrug and start emptying the display case to take the leftovers to the food bank. We don't have much, but there are a few things that someone can enjoy.

When it's time to close up, I turn to the door and feel my heart stop when Callum Wakefield walks in, looking cool as a cucumber in khaki cargo shorts and a black T-shirt. The cotton hugs the muscles in his arms, showing off his ink spectacularly, and I immediately remember what it feels like to have those arms locked around my naked body as we writhe together.

I shake my head, knocking that image away, and frown at the stupidly sexy prince.

"I'm closed for the day."

"The door was still open," he points out and smiles at me.

"I was just about to lock it."

Just like that day when you came in here and had your way with me.

But I'll be damned if I ever mention that day to him. Jerk.

"You're quite lovely when you're annoyed."

I sigh and lean on the counter. "Callum. What on earth do you want?"

"I don't want anything," he says at last, shaking his head.

"Then why are you here?"

"Excellent question." He rubs his hand over his face, showing agitation for the first time since I met him. "Because I'm a bloody glutton for punishment? I don't know, I just arrived in town, and I wanted to see you. I know I said I'd leave you be, and I will. I just wanted to see you."

"Why?"

I lean a hip against the counter and cross my arms over my chest, mostly so I don't run to him and have my way with him. I may despise him, but that doesn't mean I don't want to get him naked.

I know what that's like, and it's more than fine.

But it will never happen again.

"You've been in my head for a long time," he admits finally. His brown eyes roam over me like he's a starving animal.

The look warms me, but that comment pisses me right off.

"Right." I nod once and glance at my clean floor,

then back up at him. "I'm so memorable that you freaking *forgot*."

I clamp my mouth shut. I refuse to go through this again. It's been *years*. There's no need to rehash it.

"Aspen, I've tried to apologize to you time and time again. You won't listen, and it's bloody ridiculous."

"Ridiculous?" I stare at him as if he's lost his damn mind because he clearly has.

He swears under his breath and props his hands on his hips.

"You're right," he says, holding his hands up in surrender. "You're absolutely right. I was a wanker before. All I ask is that you hear me out."

I tilt my head to the side. Maybe, just maybe, if I let him have his say, he'll leave me alone.

"Go ahead."

"I'd been on an airplane for well over twelve hours that morning. Ellie wanted to come here for coffee, and I agreed. I'd had a shitty few weeks in Scotland, where it seemed everything that could go wrong, did. I had a lot on my mind."

I raise a brow.

"Obviously, not too much that I should have forgotten that I had been intimate with you. And I remembered right away when I sat down with Ellie. I felt horrible. I still do. I'm very sorry."

I exhale and shrug my shoulders. "Apology accepted."

Now, go away.

"Thank you," he says. "Would you like to—?"

"No." I shake my head, my voice firm. "No, I don't."

His jaw clenches as if he's frustrated all over again. "Have a good stay in Cunningham Falls, Callum."

I turn my back to him and wait. Finally, I hear his footsteps, the bell on the door, and then he's gone.

I let out a long breath.

My emotions are already raw this week. I had no idea that Callum was coming to town with the rest of the family. If I'd known, I would have tried to prepare myself. Because that was just awful.

I accepted the apology because Ellie's my friend, and I don't want things to be weird.

But Callum and I aren't going to be anything to each other. I'm not going to hang out with him. No dinners.

No sex.

But I can't carry around the anger anymore either. It's exhausting and a waste of time. It's a lesson learned, and now we move on.

Because I refuse to give up my friendship with Ellie.

I'll be cordial with Callum. That's the word. Cordial.

I can be cordial.

CHAPTER 2

~CALLUM~

"Get some rest, David," I say to my personal security when we reach my brother Sebastian's home. "I'll see you later."

"Yes, sir. Just ring me if you need anything. I do believe Alice is making dinner for the family."

"Then I'll see you at dinner," I reply with a smile.

David's been with me for several years. He's only two years older than me and is excellent at his job. He's also in wonderful shape, which I need because I like to run, and David can keep up with me.

He married Alice last year. Since then, she's become our personal chef, and it allows her to travel with us when we take lengthy holidays like this one.

The royal family demands a lot of its employees, but we are also mindful that they're people with families of their own. If we can accommodate them, we do our best.

Happy staff is *good* staff.

And David has become a mate, as well.

Liam and Ellie are staying in their new house up on Whitetail Mountain. It looks out over the lake—the whole valley, actually. So, I'm staying here at Sebastian's lake home, in the flat above the boathouse.

It's modern and more than comfortable.

Best of all, it's private.

I round the corner of the house and almost run smack dab into Ellie.

"Oh, hello," she says. "I wasn't expecting to run into you."

"Likewise. I thought you and Liam were up at the mountain house."

"We are," she says with a grin. "I just came down to chat with Nina for a bit. Liam wanted to see the security men. You can take the man out of the job, but you can't take the job out of the man."

I nod. Liam used to be the head of security for the Montana property. That was before he fell in love with and married my baby sister.

But he continues to check in with the men.

"I'm sure he has tight security up at your place, as well."

"It's borderline ridiculous, but you know how it goes."

I nod and shove my hands into my pockets. "Are you coming down here for dinner? Alice is cooking."

"She doesn't have to do that when we're all knackered with jet lag," Ellie says with a frown. "But I'd be lying if I said I wasn't relieved. Hiring Alice was the best thing we ever did."

"Agreed."

Ellie narrows her eyes and looks me over. "You look more than jet-lagged. You look cross."

I shake my head. "I'm not angry, darling."

"You are," she insists. "What's wrong? We just arrived."

I blow out a breath and stare down at the lake.

"Wait. Did you go see Aspen?" she asks.

"Why do you ask?"

"Because she's the only one who has this effect on you. It's absolutely fascinating."

"I'm happy to entertain you."

She laughs, and I feel my jaw tighten more.

"Okay, but seriously," Ellie says, losing the smile, "did you apologize?"

"Yes."

"And did she accept your apology?"

"She did."

Ellie raises a brow in surprise. "Wow, that's progress. Why do you look like you're ready to punch someone, then?"

"I tried to ask her out to dinner, and she shut me down."

My sister closes her eyes and shakes her head as if I'm totally daft.

"You're my brother, and I love you, but you're a bloody idiot."

"Hey."

"Did you think you could apologize to her and then try to score with her again? Callum, Aspen is one of my *friends*. I need you to not only make things right with her but *keep* things right. I adore her, and you've made it awkward."

"This isn't all about you, you know."

"I'm not the one who messed up," she reminds me. "And I refuse to be the one punished because my brother can't remember who he's—"

"Okay, okay. She accepted my apology. Everything should be fine."

Ellie props her hands on her hips. "Did she *really* accept, or did she simply placate you so you'd go away?"

Is that what she did? Do I still feel so bloody unsettled because Ellie's hit the nail on the head?

Bollocks.

"If she shooed you out of the shop, I'd say it was the latter," my sister continues.

I sigh. "She's impossible."

"Honestly, I don't blame her for being so angry with you. If I'd been intimate with someone and they forgot the next time they saw me, I might punch them."

"You always were violent."

"It was a dick move, as the Americans say. Sometimes, an apology isn't just about the words, Callum. *Prove* that you regret your actions."

"How in the hell am I supposed to do that? Everything I do irritates the bloody piss out of her."

"The women you've been with have made life way too easy for you. It's not hard," she says and rolls her eyes. "Start simple. Perhaps a bouquet would be a nice olive branch."

I shrug, thinking it over. "You're probably right."

"You need to try. And make it work, Callum. I love her, and she deserves for you to be nice to her."

"I wasn't *mean* to her!"

"You know what I mean. Be a gentleman. I'm having dinner and drinks with her and the other girls tomorrow night. So, if you could please take care of this before then, I'd appreciate it."

"You're a pain in my arse."

She smiles brightly. "Of course, I am. I'll see you at dinner."

She waves and walks away, and I stroll down the path to the boathouse. I key in the code to the door and walk up the steps to the loft.

The kitchen is white and inviting and open to a living space with a fireplace. Big, sliding glass doors open to a vast deck with the best view of the lake.

I retrieve a lager from the fridge and walk out to get some fresh air. Boats pepper the water, and birds fly overhead. It's a peaceful spot.

Perhaps I should buy a place of my own here. A getaway to escape to and unwind. I'll have to look into it. Nina's sister-in-law, Jenna, is an expert in local real estate.

I'll ask her some questions later.

In the meantime, this boathouse is a far cry from the palace, and it's absolutely perfect.

I wasn't going to join the others for this trip. Unlike my siblings, I don't have ties to Montana.

Actually, that's not true.

But the one tie I do have here doesn't want anything to do with me.

And yet, I can't let her go.

Is it my competitive nature that won't let it rest? Is it the challenge?

That could be a factor, but it's not all of it. I know that much.

Aspen is beautiful, intelligent, and kind. That afternoon with her a couple of years ago has replayed in my mind nearly every time I close my eyes.

How could I have been such a tosser when I saw her again last year? So careless?

I'm a lot of things, but that's not one of them. And, yes, I have a womanizing reputation, but the truth would disappoint the public.

Sure, I've had my share of bedmates, but not nearly as many as the media portrays.

I'm much more selective than that.

And since I had sex with Aspen just that one time,

the number of women I've been intimate with has been a resounding *zero.*

And despite her despising me, the chemistry I feel when I'm in the same room as Aspen is still there. I thought my skin would catch on fire this afternoon.

But is pursuing her worth the burn?

I don't know. All I know for certain is that I need to make sure I make things right with her. Not just for Ellie's sake—although that certainly factors in.

But also for me.

I hurt her.

And now, I'm here to mend things, even if that means leaving Montana without Aspen in my life.

∽

I'M EMBARRASSED TO ADMIT, even to myself, that I've never given a woman flowers before.

I've had them sent, of course. My assistant has a florist on call, and they handle my flower deliveries.

But I've never given a woman a bouquet in person.

Does that make me an arsehole?

Quite possibly.

"I'll be right out," I say to David, but he shakes his head.

"I'm going in with you, sir."

I frown.

"It's the middle of the day, and we don't know who's inside. I'll hang back."

I shrug and walk into Drips & Sips. It's a busy early afternoon. The smell of coffee hangs in the air, and the conversation of the patrons is loud.

But as I look around the room, I don't see Aspen.

So, I approach the counter and smile at a curvy blonde standing at the cash register.

Her blue eyes widen when she sees me, but I don't give her a chance to get tongue-tied.

"I'm looking for Aspen."

"Oh." Her mouth opens and closes. "She's not here."

"Do you know where she is?" I ask as I glance at the name tag on her apron. "Gretchen."

"It's her day off," the woman replies. "I don't think I'm allowed to tell you where she is."

I smile. "Of course. Thank you."

I turn to David and raise a brow.

"We have her address," he confirms as we walk back out to the car. David drives us through town, turns onto an unpaved driveway, and parks in front of a white farmhouse.

A Honda Pilot is parked in the drive in front of the garage.

I get out of the car, walk up to the front door, and ring the bell, but there's no answer.

"She has to be home," I mumble. "Her car is here."

David stands by our vehicle, surveilling the property.

There are no other homes close by. It looks like Aspen owns a nice piece of property.

Just as I'm about to return to the car, I hear a voice from around the house.

David makes a move to walk with me, but I shake my head. "Please, wait here."

He nods, and I circle the dwelling, then come to a complete stop and feel the smile spread over my face.

I'm damn glad I told David to wait.

Aspen is in a red tank top and little denim shorts, and she's bent over a flowerbed, pulling weeds and singing.

I see she's wearing Beats over her ears. Her rear moves side to side in time with the music as she sings an Ed Sheeran song.

Horribly.

"Kiss me under the light of a thousand stars..."

Singing isn't her talent. And it's ridiculously adorable.

Aspen sits back on her heels and adjusts the ugly straw hat on her head, keeping the sun off of her lovely face. She stretches her arms above her.

And when she opens her eyes and looks my way, she screeches.

"Holy shit!"

She pulls the headphones off, the hat tumbling with them, and then hurries to her feet.

I notice she's filthy from head to toe.

And I've never wanted to kiss someone so bloody badly before.

"I'm sorry to startle you," I say, holding up a hand. "You didn't hear me approach."

"Ed Sheeran was in my ear," she mumbles.

"Yes, I heard."

She cringes. "I'm a horrible singer."

So horrible.

"You're not that bad," I lie.

"Dogs cry in terror when I sing."

I can't help but laugh. "Okay, it wasn't Grammy-worthy."

"How can I help you, Callum?" she asks as she pushes a lock of that gorgeous red hair out of her face.

"I came to apologize again. And to give you these."

I pass the bouquet to her and watch as her green eyes soften as she takes in the pink and white roses. She buries her nose in them, fussing over them.

Ellie was right about the flowers.

"I accepted your apology yesterday," she reminds me but doesn't look up from the roses.

"Did you?"

Her eyes fly to mine.

"You said the words, yes. But I suspect you were just saying what I wanted to hear so I'd go away."

She tips her head to the side and watches me, then glances down at the roses again.

"Come on inside so I can put these in water before they wilt in the sun."

I don't argue. Aspen leads me up onto a beautiful

deck attached to the back of the house, and then straight into a beautiful, modern kitchen.

"Do you use those outbuildings for anything?" I ask, referring to the barn and paddock I saw not far from the house.

"No," she says. "I have some things stored in the barn, but I don't have animals. I'm too busy at the café. But I do have gardens. I'm just getting them ready for winter."

"Already? The weather's still beautiful."

"It'll be October in a few days. That means the weather can change on a dime. I'd rather get the work done now while I can still enjoy the sunshine."

She fills a vase with water, sets the roses inside, and then steps back, smiling at them.

If I'd known roses would work, I would have tried this years ago.

Make a note of this, Callum.

"You really didn't have to go to this trouble," she says as she sets her hat and headphones on the countertop.

"It was no trouble," I insist, drinking her in. That riot of red hair is tamed in a loose braid down her back. Her skin is tanned from a full summer of sunshine, and her muscles are toned.

She's fit. Athletic.

But also soft and curvy in all the right places.

I clear my throat as my blood courses through my veins.

"I won't keep you," I say. "I can see you're busy, and it's your day off."

Her eyes narrow.

"My first stop was Drips & Sips."

She nods. "Makes sense. Did Gretchen tell you to find me here?"

"No. She actually wouldn't tell me where you were."

Her lips tip up.

"You have loyal employees, Aspen."

"Damn right, I do."

"David had your address," I elaborate.

"Why would David have my address?"

"Because you're of interest to me," I reply as her eyes narrow. "And that means my security looked into you."

"Not sure I like that."

"That I'm interested, or that they looked?"

"Both?"

I smile, and to my surprise, she smiles back.

"Well, it's just an address. Without it, I wouldn't have been able to bring you these." I point to the roses.

She glances at the flowers. "And wouldn't that have been a shame?"

"Indeed."

She laughs, and the sound washes over me. Aspen has a laugh designed to seduce.

"Well, thanks. Really. I guess I should get in the shower and pull myself together. The girls are coming over later for dinner."

"Ellie mentioned it," I reply. "She's looking forward to it. I'm planning to spend my evening on the water."

"You like to boat?" she asks, surprise in her voice.

"Very much. You?"

She shakes her head. "No. I'm not a fan. But I hope you have a good time. Thanks again for the flowers."

I turn to leave but then face her again. "Does this mean I'm *really* forgiven? Or are you just being polite?"

She smiles. "It's okay, Callum."

"It's not okay." I shake my head. "And it's a mistake I regret very much."

"Thank you," she says. "You're forgiven. Truly."

"Brilliant. Enjoy your evening."

I walk out the back door so I can take in Aspen's property before I leave. The red barn is in excellent condition, and there are several other outbuildings. Her yard is large but well-maintained. I can see now that she has, in fact, cleaned out her gardening beds to ready them for winter.

I walk around the house and find David still standing by the car.

"I trust it went well?" he asks.

"Finally, yes. It went well."

CHAPTER 3

~ASPEN~

I have plenty of time, and I need to get out of the house. Because every time I walk into the kitchen, all I can see is Callum standing there, looking tall and sexy and smiling at me as if he can't get enough of me.

He brought me flowers. And it may sound silly, but fresh flowers are my weakness. If a man's willing to keep coming back to apologize, he deserves some grace.

It doesn't mean any more than that.

I was restless after my shower, and with a couple of hours to spare before the girls arrive, I decided to spend a little time at the farmer's market in Frontier Park. It's my favorite part of the week, and the summer is winding down, meaning the farmer's market won't be happening for much longer this year.

I have my large tote bag slung over my shoulder so I

can carry all of my finds, and my sunglasses are perched on my nose. My hair is up in a bun, out of my face.

When you have naturally curly hair, it constantly gets in the way. I can't even count how many times I've wanted to shave my head over the years, but then I hear Emma's little voice.

I love your hair, Mama. When will mine be long like yours?

I can't cut it.

The market is busy, as usual, with a live country band in the center of the park on a stage. Vendor tables and tents circle the perimeter and offer everything from farm-fresh produce to baked goods and artwork. The food trucks at the edge of the park serve any kind of cuisine a person might crave.

I'll grab a taco on my way out and conveniently forget to tell the girls later.

I'm not the kind of monster who passes up a taco.

I pay for a bunch of fresh mint and tuck it into my bag. When I turn to wander to the next table, I hear him.

"Anything you come up with will be perfect."

I glance to my left, and sure enough, Callum is standing next to a pretty blonde in a blue hat. David, Callum's security, stands a few feet back from them, scanning the crowd.

"I just absolutely *adore* these strawberries," the woman says, choosing four baskets full of the fruit.

"This should be enough. I'll put them in the pancakes in the morning."

"I can't wait," Callum says and tugs playfully on her hat.

Holy shit.

Of course, he's with someone. That shouldn't surprise me. Callum's a handsome man. A *single*, handsome prince. He can date anyone he wants.

I've repeatedly brushed him off and told him no.

I don't want him.

I sigh as I look down at a table full of homemade greeting cards for sale.

Then why am I jealous?

It's absolutely ridiculous. I'm *not* jealous. I'm surprised, that's all.

Not wanting to be noticed by Callum and his new girlfriend, I turn to walk in the other direction.

"Aspen?"

Fuck. Didn't make it.

I paste a smile on my lips and turn around.

"Oh, hi there."

"What a lovely surprise," Callum says. "You remember David."

"Of course." I nod at the other man. "I don't want to intrude."

"Don't be silly. This lovely woman is Alice, David's new wife."

David's wife.

"It's wonderful to meet you," Alice says, holding out

her hand for mine. "Ellie's spoken so fondly of you. I cook for the family when they travel. When I heard about this market, I just had to come and see it. This produce is simply divine."

"I agree," I say with a smile. "I had to come to get some fresh mint for our mojitos later."

"For your girls' evening," Alice says. "Of course. Ellie asked me to make my bacon roly-polies for you to nibble on tonight, and I'm going to send some fresh strawberry ice cream with marinated strawberries on top for you ladies to enjoy."

I blink at Alice, completely surprised.

"Wow," I say at last. "That sounds incredible."

"It will be," David says, smiling at his wife. "Alice's creations are out of this world."

Callum shoves his hands into his pockets and grins at me in that way he did earlier today that made me want to climb him like a tree.

I seriously need to get my mind out of the gutter.

"Well, you'd better come eat it with us," I say to Alice.

"Oh, I couldn't do that. I don't want to crash your party."

"You're not crashing," I say. "You're invited. And I am looking forward to chatting more later. I want to hear all about your wedding, and I can't wait to eat that ice cream. I'd better finish up here so I can get home and chop this mint."

"Don't chop," Alice says. "Tear it. The flavor will be better."

"See? I'm learning from you already."

She smiles brightly, and I immediately like Alice very much.

"Have a good evening, gentlemen," I say with a nod and quickly walk away. I wander through the rest of the market, but my heart's not in it anymore. I can't get Callum and his sexy smile out of my head.

Damn him.

I'm not angry with him anymore. Not really. His apology was sincere, and I'm ready to move on.

But why do I have to run into him all the damn time? Forgetting about Callum Wakefield is hard enough on its own. Seeing him around town only makes it harder.

I sigh and admire some silver earrings, then decide to buy them for myself before heading home.

I'm excited to see my friends this evening. We don't get together as often as we'd like. And tonight, we have Ellie back in town.

With a new friend to join us, as well.

It'll be fun.

～

"I'VE NEVER HAD anything this good in my mouth before," Natasha says as she scoops another bite of strawberry ice cream past her lips.

"I know, right?" Monica agrees. "And these berries are *amazing*. What is on them?"

"I soaked them for about an hour in balsamic vinegar," Alice replies and sips her third mojito. "This has been so much fun. Thank you for inviting me. I know it's odd for the staff to hang out with the royals, Your Highness, so if this is inappropriate, please just let me know."

"I invited you, too," Ellie says with a laugh. "I think you know by now that we think of our employees as our friends. I'm so glad you came with me tonight. And when we're not in an official setting, you can call me Ellie."

"Yes, ma'am," Alice says and then joins us when we laugh. "I mean, Ellie."

My mind is a little fuzzy around the edges from too many mojitos and a *lot* of food. But I wouldn't change a thing. This is my tribe. It's taken a lot of years to get here, and I'm loving every minute of it.

"Aspen?" Ellie says.

"Hmm?"

"On a scale of one to passed out cold, how drunk are you?"

I snicker. "I'm a solid five. Leaning toward six." I take a sip of my drink. "There we go, I'm a six."

"Excellent. I have a request. A favor, if you will."

I frown. "Anything for you, Ellie, you know that."

She bites her lip. "It's a big ask."

"Consider it done," I insist, curious now what Princess Eleanor could possibly need from me.

"Well, you know the annual hospital benefit that's happening next weekend?" Ellie asks. "Our family has been invited because we donated some funds to the new imaging department."

"Do you need help finding a dress?" I ask her and then purse my numb lips. "Willa has some stuff at Dress It Up. I'll go with you. I need a few things anyway."

"No, that's not it," Ellie says, shaking her head. "Are you going to the benefit?"

"I hadn't planned on it."

"We have an extra seat at our table, and I need you to go with Callum."

I frown. "Why?"

"Because it'll be fun. It's not a date," she hurries to assure me. "I just need you to go on a date with my brother."

"But it's not a date."

"Not at all."

I see Natasha and Monica exchange a look over their mojitos. Alice is busy scooping us more ice cream.

"You said *anything* I need," Ellie reminds me.

"Yeah, I thought maybe you needed some scones or coffee or something."

"I need scones," Monica says. "Huckleberry ones."

"Me, too," Natasha adds.

"Oh, I'd love to try those. We don't have huckleberries in the UK," Alice says.

"Focus," Ellie says. "Please say you'll go, Aspen."

Ellie bats those ridiculous lashes at me, and I know I'm a sucker.

I can't tell her no.

"I'm not supposed to be dating Callum," I mutter with a frown.

"We missed something," Monica says. "Something good. And you'd better spill it."

Ellie's eyes almost pop out of her head. "They don't know?"

"We're about to," Natasha says. "Talk, Aspen."

"I slept with him," I mutter and suck down half of a mojito. "And it was damn good. And there was no sleeping done, by the way."

"Attagirl," Monica says.

"And then, the next time I saw him, he forgot all about it and me."

The room falls silent for a heartbeat, and then Natasha giggles. "What a prick."

"Hey, that's my brother," Ellie says but shrugs. "And, yes, it was dreadful, and he's a knob. But what she's leaving out is that he's spent the past two years apologizing and agonizing."

"Good," Monica says. "He should. But did you forgive him?"

"Yeah." I reach for more ice cream. "Hating him is exhausting. Also, have you seen him? He's too sexy to hate."

"Alice is awfully quiet," Natasha says. "What do you think?"

"That it's not my place to talk," she says. "Except maybe to say this. Today, after you left us at the market, he watched you for ten minutes like a lovesick puppy."

I bark out a laugh. "Right."

"He did," Alice says. "I've no reason to fib. He speaks highly of you, and he was genuinely happy to see you."

"Hmm." I eat the ice cream, thinking over everything that was said. "I guess it won't hurt to go to the benefit."

I might regret this when I'm sober.

"Brilliant," Ellie says and leans over to give me a drunk kiss on the cheek. "It'll be so fun to have you there. Now, do *you* need a dress?"

"Shit. Yeah, I'll be going to see Willa for sure."

"We'll go with you," Natasha says. "Now, give us more details about those sexy times with a certain prince."

"Must she?" Ellie asks, scrunching up her nose. "He's my *brother*. I don't want to think about it."

"She must," Monica says.

"It was a long time ago," I reply, brushing it off. "I hardly remember."

Lies. It's all lies. I remember everything.

But I don't want to share it with them. I want to keep it just for me.

"She's not gonna spill the beans," Natasha says. "Pity. I bet it's a hell of a story."

"Alice, who does your hair?" Monica asks, changing the subject. I could kiss her. I might kiss her before the night is over. My friend glances my way and winks at me.

"Oh, I go to a salon in London," Alice says and brushes her fingers through her blond locks.

"I like the length," Monica says, tilting her head to the side. "But I wonder if you'd be open to some highlights to give it a bit of depth?"

"I might be. I haven't added color in a long while."

"I own the salon downtown. If you're interested, just let me know. I'll get you on the books."

"Thank you," Alice says. "I could use a day of pampering."

"Book it," Ellie says. "And add nails, a facial, and a massage. On me, of course."

"Ellie—"

"You follow us around the world and make amazing things like this ice cream. Trust me, it's my pleasure."

Alice grins. "Well, I won't say no. Thank you."

"I want more real food," Natasha says as she stands and walks toward the kitchen. "I always eat too much when we get together, but I'll just run an extra three miles tomorrow."

"I don't run unless something's chasing me," Monica says. "And even then, it's a crapshoot."

"Where did you get these pretty flowers?" Natasha calls from the kitchen. "They look like they came from Brooke's."

I take a drink and answer without thinking. "Callum brought them to me this afternoon."

Three pairs of eyes turn to me, and Natasha pokes her head out of the kitchen to join them.

"What?"

"Callum *brought* them?" Monica asks. "He was here, in this house?"

"In the kitchen this afternoon," I confirm. "He *just* brought flowers. And asked me to forgive him again. Nothing else."

"I have to say it," Monica says with a smug grin. "The prince likes you, Aspen Calhoun."

"He felt guilty." I set my ice cream bowl aside before I gain seventy pounds. "Besides, we're not in the seventh grade."

"No, he likes you," Alice says, surprising me. Although I've only known her for a few short hours, I've learned that Alice is a woman of few words. Or maybe she's just shy, and we're new to her. "He definitely likes you."

"I thought we changed the subject."

"We did," Ellie says. "And then we discovered the flowers."

I shake my head and try to change the subject again. "What does one wear to a benefit?"

"A cocktail dress," Natasha says. "A sexy-as-fuck, knock-him-on-his-ass cocktail dress."

"That," Monica says, pointing to Natasha. "You wear that."

"I'd better get some more exercise this week and stop eating this ice cream," I murmur. "Because I kind of want to knock him on his ass."

"Attagirl," Monica says again, making me laugh.

∾

I scrunch up my nose and stare at my reflection in the dressing room mirror.

It's been twelve hours since I told Ellie I'd go to the benefit with Callum, and I'm deeply regretting that decision.

"Come, show me," Natasha says from the other side of the curtain at Dress It Up.

I step out, and her eyes narrow.

"Turn."

I comply.

"Turn again."

I roll my eyes but do as she asks.

"Next."

"I've tried on five dresses, Tash. We're running out of options in Cunningham Falls."

"Try the purple one with the low back. You look amazing in jewel tones."

"And then I'm done trying, and I'll just choose one of these. It's for *one night*. I'm not going to stress over it."

I'm totally going to stress over it. But if I say I'm not, maybe it'll come true.

I slip into the amethyst-colored dress and tilt my head to the side.

Not bad.

Probably the best one.

I walk out, and Natasha grins. "I hate that you look so damn good in the jewel tones. It's the fabulous red hair. That's gorgeous. Turn for me."

I do, and she whistles.

"That's a knock-him-on-his-ass dress," she confirms. "Wrap it up. Do you have black heels?"

"Heels? Hell, no. I'm on my feet all day, and I haven't dressed up since—"

Since my wedding day.

But I don't say that out loud.

"In a really long time."

"We'll find you some. Man, your back looks amazing in that gown. I didn't know you had a tramp stamp."

I turn and struggle to see my back in the mirror.

"I don't."

"Ha, gotcha."

I stick out my tongue at her and return to the dressing room to change into my jeans and T-shirt. After, Natasha and I walk to the counter to pay.

"This is a stunning dress," Willa says with a smile. "And it's gorgeous on you. Yeah, I peeked."

"Thanks. I need shoes."

"You've come to the right place, doll."

CHAPTER 4

~CALLUM~

The lake is clear this morning. Calm. So still, in fact, I can see a perfect reflection of the trees and homes on the opposite side of the lake in the water. A lone soul kayaks across the smooth water, the only disruption in the glass-like lake. The smell of pine is heavy in the air.

It's rare to be able to enjoy mornings like this. To not have the press camped outside, trying to snap a photo or get a word.

They'd drive a saint bloody insane.

And I'm no saint.

The longer I'm in Montana with its wide-open spaces and kind people, I understand why my siblings enjoy being here so much. It's one of the few places in the world where we have quiet. No prying eyes.

Just peace.

The sun hasn't quite risen yet, but the sky is painted

in pinks and blues, the birds chirping. When was the last time I took a minute to admire a sky and listen to birds singing the song of their kind?

I couldn't tell you.

I'm on my second cuppa of the day. I haven't been sleeping well. At first, I blamed jet lag. But I've been in town for several days now, and only one thing has been in the forefront of my mind.

Aspen Calhoun.

With her mane of fiery hair and those green eyes that can cut me in two with just one look—or set my blood to boiling in the blink of an eye.

Each time I see her, it's like a roundhouse kick to the face. She's more beautiful than my memory gives her credit for.

And I can't get her out of my mind. She's always there, both when I'm sleeping and while I'm awake.

Of course, it's just my luck that I'm attracted to a woman who doesn't want anything to do with me. Not that I can blame her. I understand her anger. I was a complete prat. But I felt like we turned a corner yesterday when she finally accepted my apology.

I check the time. I agreed to go for a run with David at seven. We usually go earlier, but I cut him some slack since he's a newlywed.

What red-blooded man wants to leave his wife so early in the morning?

I have half an hour, so I go inside, change into my running clothes, and head up to the big house to see if

Alice set out any scones or muffins for us to nibble on.

I find I'm not disappointed when I reach the kitchen and see plates of both.

I've just taken a bite of a scone when I hear my sister behind me.

"Good morning."

I turn and frown at Ellie, who's currently rubbing her sleepy eyes.

"Why are you here?"

She scowls. "We lost power up at the house last night. Someone cut down a tree, and it fell over onto some powerlines. All I know is that Liam and I slept here last night."

"Things like that don't happen in London," I comment and chew my scone. "I like it here."

"Me, too," she says. "I feel almost like a normal person here. I know we aren't, and we still have responsibilities, but for just a little while, it's nice to unwind."

Exactly what I was thinking earlier.

"I'm glad I ran into you," Ellie says and reaches for a scone. "I need to ask a huge favor."

I frown. "Are you all right?"

"Oh, yes, I'm fine. I just need something."

Ellie's my baby sister. I'd do anything in the world for her. Saying yes and asking questions later is a given.

"Name it."

She smiles but then bites her lip and looks down as if she's nervous.

"It's sort of a lot to ask."

"For fuck's sake, Eleanor, just ask already."

She sighs heavily. "Well, aren't you moody this morning? Liam and I, along with Sebastian and Nina, are attending a benefit dinner and auction for the hospital this weekend. Aspen's going to be sitting at our table, and we have an extra seat. Well, I think it would be lovely if you escorted her."

I narrow my eyes at my sister. "You've been warning me off her for years."

"No, I haven't," she says with a frown, staring at her scone. "I simply didn't want you playing with her emotions, that's all. But she's going to be at our table, and there's an available seat. It would be lovely if you joined us."

I lean on the counter and give it some thought. I've been chomping at the bit to spend time with Aspen. To get to know her better. Perhaps this would be a good opportunity to do just that.

"Aspen's not my biggest fan, Ellie."

"Well, I already mentioned the idea to her, and she was absolutely thrilled."

"Now I know you're lying."

"Okay, *thrilled* might be stretching it a bit, but she didn't hate the idea. It'll be a fun evening, Callum. You've escorted countless women to functions over the years."

I blow out a breath and check my watch. "I have to go."

"Say you'll do this. Please. For me. I never get to spend time with you, certainly not in a social setting."

"Are you sure Aspen knows and is okay with it?"

"She's perfectly fine with it," Ellie says. "I assure you. I wouldn't intentionally put either of you in an uncomfortable situation."

I shrug, nod, and wave at my sister as I hurry out to meet David on the veranda. He's already stretching.

"Good morning, Your Highness," he says. He starts every day the same way, no matter how many times I tell him to call me Callum.

"Good morning," I reply as I set my watch for an outdoor run. "Ten today?"

"Only ten miles?" David asks with a wink. "I thought for sure you'd want to go fifteen today after the long flight the other day and not much exercise since then."

Just the thought of ten miles has me exhausted.

Or maybe that's just the lack of sleep. And now that I know I'll be escorting Aspen to a function, I'll get even less rest.

Blast it.

"Is everything all right?" David asks.

"Fine," I say with a curt nod. "Let's do this."

"What's wrong with you," Sebastian asks. It's been a long day. After my run, I had business to see to until my brother rang me and invited me up to Whitetail Mountain to see our friend, Jacob, who owns the resort here. I've largely ignored the two men as I sipped my stout and admired the view of the valley below, wondering what Aspen is up to down there.

"I've no idea what you're talking about."

Sebastian and Jacob share a glance.

"You haven't said two words since you got here," Jacob says. "You're not typically a man of few words."

I rub my hand over my face and gesture for the bartender to bring me another pint. The pub is quiet this evening, so there aren't any prying eyes or cameras pointed our way. I would typically enjoy some quiet time with my brother and Jacob, a few beers and some laughs.

"Perhaps I'm still suffering from jet lag."

"Bollocks," Sebastian says. "You shake jet lag off faster than anyone I know. You went for a run this morning."

I shrug. "How's your wife?" I ask Jacob, trying to change the subject.

"Grace is perfect in every way imaginable," my friend replies with a sly smile. "Thank you for asking. Now, back to you."

I shake my head. "There's nothing to say."

I'm not looking their way. Instead, I stare straight

ahead at the wall of liquor bottles and a mirror where I can see our reflections.

They share a glance again.

"Women are bloody frustrating," I grumble and push my hand through my hair.

"And there we are," Jacob says good-naturedly and claps his hand on my shoulder. "Let's talk it out."

I shake my head and take a sip of Guinness. "I fucked up. I admit it, and I've apologized for it, for two damn years. She says she's forgiven me."

"But?" Sebastian asks.

"Something doesn't sit well," I reply. "I'm not sleeping. I can't get her off my mind."

"I've never known a woman to catch your fancy like this," Jacob says as he raises a brow. "If she's so difficult, just move on."

"Tried that," I say. "But I can't seem to stop thinking about her."

"Well, then go to London and talk with her," Jacob suggests.

I laugh and shake my head. "She's actually here, in Cunningham Falls."

Sebastian's eyes narrow. "Aspen?"

I nod.

"The new owner of Drips & Sips?" Jacob asks. "I quite like her. She's intelligent and has made good business decisions. Not to mention, she's quite lovely to look at."

I stare at my friend. "You're married to the most perfect woman in the world, remember?"

"And I'm as dedicated to her today as the day I married her. It doesn't mean I can't admire a pretty girl. So, you fucked up, and she won't speak to you?"

"She's speaking to me. Like I said, she says she's forgiven me."

"So, what's the problem?" Sebastian asks.

"I don't want her to simply forgive me. I want to get to know her better. I want to spend time with her. Ellie talked me into escorting her to the benefit this weekend."

"That's a good start," Jacob says. "Does Aspen know you're taking her?"

"According to Ellie, yes."

"Like Jacob said, it's a good start. See how the evening goes and take it from there. And, Callum, my gut tells me that she's not someone you can play with."

"No. She's not. And I'm not interested in games with her. I can't put my finger on why, but she's different. I want to figure her out."

"I don't know that we can ever figure them out," Jacob says. "I've been with Grace for a long while now, and there are still moments I feel like I don't know what the hell I'm doing."

"I'm going to try," I reply. "I'm going to convince her that I'm not a daft idiot who just wants to get in her knickers."

"You mean, you *don't* want to get in her knickers?" Jacob asks.

"Of course, I do. But that's not all I want."

"I do believe my little brother just admitted that he's going to court a woman." Sebastian raises his glass. "Cheers to that."

"Cheers indeed," Jacob says. "I'd love to be a fly on the wall."

I laugh, but inside, I'm nervous. I've never had to work for a woman's affections before. I have a feeling Aspen's going to make me work harder for this than I've ever worked for anything in my bloody life.

∽

Whenever I have something on my mind, the best way to work it out is exercise.

Now is no different.

David and I took our run yesterday and discovered a whole network of amazing paths that wind through town and along the lake. There must be hundreds of miles of them, and we decided the best way to explore them is by bicycle.

We spent the morning at a local cyclery shop and walked out with two state-of-the-art bikes that will be a joy to use. I'll simply store them at Sebastian's home for anyone who might fancy a ride.

I refuse to wear spandex. I'm not trying to win any races. Instead, we're dressed in our typical casual wardrobe of cargo shorts and T-shirts. We did invest in helmets and riding gloves, though.

There's no sense in being foolish.

The path is clean and paved as we ride along the lake, the glistening blue of the water sparkling through the trees. The foliage is changing color, going from green to orange and yellow.

It's a stellar day.

We've just passed a new home construction site when my bicycle blows a tire.

"Bloody hell," I mutter as I climb off the bike and stare at the flat. "Tell me you have a kit with you to fix this."

David, with his mouth in a thin, unhappy line, shakes his head. "Negative, sir. I didn't think to buy one. I'll just call and have someone come and get us."

"Everything okay?"

I glance back to see none other than Aspen Calhoun come riding up behind us. Her eyes widen when she recognizes us, but she slows and stops next to me.

"Flat tire."

She glances down at my tire, then hops off of her bicycle before leaning it on its kickstand and fidgeting with a small pouch under her seat.

"I can fix this," she says. "It'll only take a minute."

"I can call someone," David offers, but she's already shaking her head and squatting next to my bike.

"I'll have it done way before anyone can get here," she says. "Looks like you ran over a nail back there. I wish the construction crews were more thorough when they clean up. You're not the first person to meet this fate on this trail. Jerks."

She fiddles with something, and suddenly, my tire is full of air again.

"You'll want to replace the tire soon, but this will at least get you through today."

"Aspen."

She doesn't look me in the eyes, just returns to the pouch under her seat and stows her tools.

I grip her arm just above the elbow, and she turns those eyes up to me. She looks…*unsure.*

"Thank you. You saved the day."

"I'm not even wearing my cape." She winks and turns to go, but I'm still holding onto her, so she raises a brow and looks down at my hand, then back up to my face. "You have my arm."

"So I do." I want to kiss her so bloody badly, my lips hurt. "I didn't realize you enjoyed cycling."

"I'm just trying to soak in all of this amazing weather," she says. "Like I said the other day, it can leave in the blink of an eye around here. And I'm not a big fan of winter activities. Too cold."

"What other activities do you enjoy?" I ask.

"Let's ride and talk," she suggests, and I immediately agree, pushing off on my bike and riding next to her. David keeps a safe distance behind us, never letting me get out of sight but not listening to our conversation either.

I'm just thrilled that she didn't roll her eyes and ride away, leaving me in the dust.

"I like to hike, ride my bike, and sometimes I jog, but not if it's too hot. I do *not* like to go camping or boating."

"Why is that?"

She shrugs a shoulder. "I just don't. I pay a mortgage so I have a roof over my head. Sleeping in a tent doesn't sound fun in the least."

"No camping."

"Day trips are really all I have time for anyway. Drips & Sips is more than a full-time gig."

"When is the last time you went on holiday?"

"I've never taken a vacation."

The bike wobbles beneath me as my head whips over to stare at her, and I have to stop myself from falling.

"Never?"

"Nope."

"That's incredible."

"I don't have much time for travel."

"If you could go anywhere at all, where would you like to go?"

"The Maldives," she says without hesitation. "The photos make it look like heaven, and I heard it's sinking into the sea. I'd like to see it before it's gone."

I can take you there tonight.

I want to do just that. Whisk her away for an incredible holiday in paradise.

But I don't think she'd be open to that. Not yet.

"What about you?" she asks.

"Me?"

"Yes, is there somewhere in the world you haven't been that you'd like to visit?"

I frown, thinking it over. "I've been pretty much everywhere," I say. "Actually, there are some things in Alaska I haven't seen that I think would be fascinating."

"You could take an Alaskan cruise," she suggests. "If you like water, that is."

"I don't mind the water, but I think what I want to see would best be done on foot."

"You want to walk across Alaska?"

"Parts of it," I say with a laugh. "You look appalled."

"That doesn't sound fun at all. If I'm on vacation, I don't want to hike in the middle of nowhere. I want to sit on a gorgeous beach with a cold drink and a hot cabana boy."

I raise a brow. "Cabana boy?"

"Sure. He can fetch me things and just look good."

"Hmm." I'll make sure any servers in the Maldives who come into contact with us are female.

I'll be the only man she ogles.

"Well, this was fun, but I have to turn back," she says as she comes to a stop and takes a drink of water. "I have the afternoon shift at the café."

"You take different shifts?"

"Yeah, we rotate. It's fair that way. Although I'm

around for both shifts many days, particularly when we're shorthanded. Have a good day."

"Wait."

She stops and raises a brow at me.

"What time shall I pick you up on Saturday?"

"I'll just meet you there."

"That's not how this works. If I'm escorting you, I'll pick you up."

She bites her lip, and just when I think she's about to say *no*, she says, "Seven works."

"I'll see you on Saturday at seven, then. Have a good day, Aspen."

She waves. "You, too."

I watch her ride away, her ass sitting perfectly on her seat. For the first time in too bloody long, I feel hope catch in my chest.

I can't wait for Saturday.

CHAPTER 5

~ASPEN~

"I would kill for your hair," Monica says as she takes my red curls from a riot of craziness to a sexy, sleek, and sophisticated 'do.

"And I'd kill to have you live with me so it looks like this every day. Because, trust me, it doesn't. It's usually a frizzy mess."

"Nonsense," Monica says. "It's not frizzy at all because your best friend made you start using decent hair products to keep it tamed. You're welcome, by the way."

"Your makeup has never looked better," Natasha says, stepping back to take a look at her handiwork. Both of my friends came over to help me get ready for this charity event, where apparently, I've been roped into going as Callum's date.

I'm still not entirely sure how that happened, except that I'm doing Ellie a solid.

That's right, it's for Ellie.

"When do I get to see?" I ask.

"Perfection takes a minute," Monica says as she continues fussing with my hair. Natasha comes at me with yet another brush.

"I don't need perfection," I reply. "I just need: *I don't look like Quasimodo.*"

"Oh, honey, we can do much better than that," Natasha says. With a final stroke of the brush, she stands back and grins from ear to ear. "I'm damn good."

"I mean, was I horrible to begin with?"

I hope not. I don't usually wear a lot of makeup.

"Of course, not. You're gorgeous. I just accentuated what was already there," Natasha says. "This is all you."

"And your brushes," I add.

"I'm done, too," Monica says and reaches for the mirror. "You, my love, are an absolute knockout."

"Yeah, yeah, let me see."

She turns the mirror to me, and I just stare at myself for a moment. I didn't look this good on my wedding day. Sure, I was seventeen, hugely pregnant, and flat broke, but still.

"See? She's speechless," Natasha says with satisfaction.

"Wow."

"No, wow is going to be when you get this dress on," Monica says and turns toward my closet where the dress in question hangs on the front of the door. "If

Callum's jaw doesn't hit the floor, he's not a red-blooded man."

"That's what I told her," Natasha says. "Also, it's a good thing there will be a lot of doctors at the gala tonight because the back on this dress will give most of the men in attendance heart failure."

"You two are way too good for my ego," I laugh as I carefully strip out of my loose tank top and shorts and reach for the dress, not caring in the least that I'm mostly naked in front of these girls.

They've seen me at my *most* naked—when I was broken and crying or scared and unsure. Physically nude is nothing in comparison.

I slip into the amethyst-colored gown and turn in a circle for my friends to see.

"Holy Mary, mother of God," Monica breathes. "I would give up both ovaries to be able to wear a dress like that. And I'm trying to get pregnant."

"Same," Natasha says with a sigh. "Except for the pregnant part. Because, *no.*"

I turn and look at my back in the mirror. "You guys, it's literally millimeters away from my ass crack. That can't be okay. What if I sit down, and it pulls a certain way, and you can see my crack?"

"You're a grown woman," Monica says with a scowl. "Sit carefully. If a light breeze hits your crack, readjust."

I roll my eyes. "Great. Also, I didn't know you and your husband were trying to get pregnant."

"It's a new thing," Monica says with a shrug. "I was

afraid if I talked about it, it might jinx it. But you're my best friends, and a girl has to talk about this stuff."

"It's gonna happen," Natasha says with a sage nod. "You just have to bone him like...all the time."

"Well, that's never been an issue," Monica says with a laugh. "But enough about me. Aspen, you're stunning, and I almost hate you for it."

"Speaking of boning," Natasha says, "you're *so* gonna get some tonight, Aspen. He won't be able to keep his hands off you."

"I'm *not* sleeping with him," I insist, shaking my head. "This is a favor for Ellie. I'll be cordial, I'll enjoy Ellie and Nina, and then I'll come home. No sex. No flirting."

"Well, that's damn boring," Monica says. "He's a *prince* for fuck's sake, and he's clearly into you. At least flirt a little. You owe it to all of the other women in the world to take one for the team here."

"You're sick," I reply with a laugh. These two *always* make me laugh, calm my nerves, and make me feel like there's nothing I can't do.

They're the reason I got up the nerve to buy Drips & Sips in the first place, rather than being content just working there. Monica and Natasha are the best friends a girl could ask for.

The doorbell rings, and I freeze.

"Awesome, we get to watch him swallow his tongue," Natasha says with an excited little shimmy as she takes one final look at me and then gestures for me to follow Monica to the door.

Callum has just stepped inside, holding flowers, and is smiling at something Monica said when his eyes shift, and he catches sight of me.

"Totally just swallowed his tongue," Natasha whispers in my ear and then steps away. Callum's eyes are round, and he has to take a moment to swallow hard. It gives me time to take him in. He's wearing a black suit with a white shirt and a blue tie. He's just so...*hot.* Square jawline, dark hair and eyes, and when he clenches his jaw in the way he's doing now, I want to leap on him and kiss him.

But this is a favor for Ellie. Nothing more.

"Are you still punishing me, then?" he asks.

"What do you mean?"

"You'll have me on my knees, begging for mercy before the evening is over."

I laugh, but his eyes tell me he's not kidding.

"Thank you. You look dashing yourself."

He grins and steps toward me. "I remembered how much you like flowers."

Pink roses this time, and I can't resist burying my nose in them to fuss over the blooms for just a moment.

"They're lovely."

"I'm happy to put those in water for you before we go," Monica says, taking the flowers from me. "You two should be on your way."

"Thanks for everything," I reply. "Just let yourselves out whenever and lock up as you go."

I turn to retrieve the little clutch purse Natasha lent me for the evening and hear Callum's sharp inhale and a whispered, "Jesus, help me."

I spin back to him. "What happened? Are you hurt?"

He shakes his head. "Yes. I'm going to have to beat every man at this thing tonight off with a bloody stick. My God, Aspen, you're a vision."

Okay, he says some nice things. And the way he's looking at me makes me long for stuff I've already experienced with him.

But we're not going there.

"I'm sure you say that to all the girls."

He doesn't reply as we say goodbye to my friends and walk to his car, where David and a driver wait.

Once we're in the backseat, Callum takes my hand and kisses my knuckles, making my stomach jolt in surprise and pleasure.

"No, Aspen. I don't say that to all the girls. You're absolutely gorgeous, and I'm a lucky man to have you as my date tonight."

I want to sigh. I want to climb on his lap.

Instead, I simply smile and silently thank Natasha for talking me into this dress.

"I HAD no idea there would be so many people here," Nina says as she surveys the room. "Cunningham Falls is such a small town."

"But a strong community," I remind her. "And a proud one."

I'm not surprised in the least that this ballroom is full. We're seated near the stage where the mayor will step up a little later and announce the winners of the silent auction, currently going on at the opposite side of the room. Sebastian, Callum, and Liam are over there browsing the items up for bid as Nina, Ellie, and I enjoy a glass of champagne and a chance to chat.

"Your dress should be illegal," Nina says with a wink. "Or maybe just looking that hot in it should be."

"It's divine," Ellie agrees. "Who is the designer?"

I blink at her. "I have no idea. I bought it at Dress It Up."

"Willa keeps such wonderful things in that boutique," Nina says with a sigh.

I eye both of their gowns. Nina's sparkles with white stones on the bodice. It's strapless, so she's paired it with a gorgeous sapphire necklace.

And Ellie is as beautiful as ever in a one-shouldered pink dress that shows off her figure perfectly.

"Do I want to know the designers of your gowns?" I ask.

"Valentino," Ellie says.

"Givenchy," Nina adds with a wink. "And yours just slayed both of ours. It's not always about the label, but the body wearing it. And with a form like yours, you'd look amazing in a burlap sack."

I snort and take another sip of my champagne, grateful that these wonderful women are welcoming and kind without an elitist bone in their bodies.

Nina is married to Callum's eldest brother, Sebastian. And Ellie is Callum's younger sister. Royals literally surround me at this event.

Who in the world do I imagine I am, thinking I belong at a table with the royal family?

"Uh-oh," Ellie says. "You have a look. What's wrong?"

"It's a little disconcerting realizing you're surrounded by royals."

"Friends," Nina says with a shake of her head. "We're your friends, Aspen."

"I know." I sip my champagne. "And I love that you are. But every once in a while, I realize that I'm sitting with British royalty, and it knocks me back for a minute."

"I understand," Nina says with a grin. "It still surprises me sometimes, too. But at the root of it all, we're women."

I nod and want to ask some questions about the royal life, but the guys return before I have a chance to reply. Callum sits next to me and wraps his arm around my back.

"Do you need anything?" he asks. "A fresh drink? Something to eat?"

"No, thank you. Did you find anything good over there?" I indicate the auction table.

"A few things," he says. "The offerings are impressive."

"World-class," Sebastian agrees. He should know, he's a prince, after all.

Before long, dinner is served. People stop by the table to say hello or to gush about the royal family and say how they enjoy seeing the family around town. I notice odd looks coming my way, but I do my best to ignore them.

Yes, I'm aware that I'm at this table. I'm also aware that I don't belong.

But I'll be damned if I'll let it ruin my evening. I'm having more fun than I expected. Even Callum has been engaging, funny, and attentive. He's hardly annoyed me at all. And his fingers have found their way down my spine a couple of times, setting my nerves on fire.

Maybe this dress was a mistake, after all. Because I'm as turned on as I've ever been in my life.

"Ladies and gentlemen," Mayor Jeffries begins, and the room quiets so we can listen. Callum's fingers don't leave my spine. He masterfully tickles the flesh on my back, but his face is non-expressive and turned to the mayor as if he's not doing anything at all. I want to squirm, but that would be too obvious and garner attention, so I sit still and will my libido to take a chill pill.

"Thank you for being with us tonight to celebrate the completion of the new diagnostics unit in the Cunningham Falls Medical Center. Because of your generosity, our community will have the best in diagnostic imaging and may even save some lives."

The room erupts in applause.

"We're here tonight as a community to celebrate and to continue donations toward our medical community so we can stay on the cutting edge of medical technology and ensure that our friends and family stay as healthy as possible. As you know, there has been a silent auction going on in the back of the room all evening. It's now officially closed. I have the honor of announcing tonight's winners."

More applause as someone passes a spreadsheet to the mayor.

"Let's get started, shall we? First up, we have a first-class, all-expenses-paid vacation to Fiji. This includes accommodations at a five-star resort and first-class travel."

Mayor Jeffries waggles his eyebrows.

"Sounds fancy, doesn't it? Well, it looks like His Royal Highness, Callum Wakefield placed the highest bid for this item. Congratulations, sir."

My gaze whips to Callum, who simply nods while the rest of the room applauds.

"You bought a vacation?"

"It's for a very good cause," he says. "And a certain someone I know told me she's dreamt of a tropical holiday. Granted, it's not the Maldives, but that wasn't one of the options."

I stare at him in disbelief.

"You bought me a *vacation?*"

He reaches to take my hand, but I immediately pull it away. The mayor is still announcing winners, the room applauds, but I can't hear anything over the rush of blood in my ears.

"Excuse me," I murmur and stand to leave. I need a minute to catch my breath. To decide if I want to kill him or kiss him.

I've just rounded the corner of the restrooms, pushed inside, and leaned on the counter to hang my head and gulp in air when the door flings open behind me, and Callum comes waltzing in as if he owns the place.

"This is a women's restroom."

"I'm aware," he says, watching me closely. "Tell me why you ran."

"You bought me a vacation, Callum."

He blows out a breath. "I did, yes."

"I didn't ask for one."

He narrows his eyes at me. "You don't have to ask for something for me to buy it for you."

"You shouldn't be buying me *anything*," I say in frustration. "I told you I forgive you. What are you trying to do now? Buy me expensive things to help assuage your guilt?"

He steps toward me and cages me against the counter without touching me.

"I was doing something kind. It was spur of the moment. I'm not trying to *buy you*, as you so crudely put it. I'm trying to enjoy something with you. Because if you think I'll let anyone but me enjoy your first holiday with you, you're out of your bloody mind, darling."

I sigh, completely confused. Now he wants to take trips with me?

I move to walk past him. "We should get back."

"Aspen."

My name on his lips stops me.

"I just want to enjoy something with you. It's as simple as that."

I nod once, resolved to figuring this all out later when I don't have friends and a room full of people I know waiting. They all saw me leave, and likely saw Callum chase after me.

"We'll talk about it later."

I know that doesn't satisfy him, but he backs away and allows me to walk out of the restroom ahead of him. He follows me back to the table, where we listen to the rest of the auction announcements and eat dessert as people get up to make speeches.

Finally, we're on our way back to my house.

"You bought me a vacation," I say again when we're safely tucked in the car's backseat.

"Clearly, that displeases you," Callum says with a sigh. "It wasn't meant as an insult, Aspen. I saw it on the table, remembered our conversation the other day, and thought it would be fun to take a holiday with you. We can go whenever you like, whenever it fits your schedule."

"I just don't know how we went from polite acquaintances to taking trips together in the span of one evening." I sigh and look over at him, surprised when I see him looking down at me with dark eyes full of apprehension. Hurt? Confusion?

Is Callum as confused as I am?

"Thank you," I say at last and reach over for his hand, which engulfs mine perfectly. "I don't mean to sound rude or ungrateful. It took me by surprise. Given our history, I wouldn't think we'd make good travel partners."

"Things change," he murmurs before bringing my hand to his lips to kiss my knuckles as the car pulls into my driveway.

I'm exhausted when the door to the car finally opens, and Callum takes my hand to escort me up to the front door.

"I'm not going to ask you in," I inform him.

"Of course, not," he murmurs. His forearm rests on the door, and his fingers play with some of my curls. "Your hair looks like fire."

"It was super annoying when I was a teenager and already didn't fit in."

"It's beautiful. Just like the rest of you. This dress is

every fantasy I've ever had, draped around you like sin."

I swallow hard. "You're good with words."

"I'm not, no," he replies softly. "And I'm not one to use pretty platitudes. I'm simply telling you the truth."

His hand slips down my arm and around to my back, where his fingertips glide up my spine. The touch is more thorough and seductive than earlier, moving from just above my ass to my neck.

Goosebumps break out over my flesh. I couldn't hide them if I wanted to.

"You're beautiful," he murmurs just before his lips cover mine. The combination of his fingers on my back and his lips on mine is intoxicating. I feel like I'm floating as he deepens the kiss, sweeping that magical tongue across the seam of my lips and into my mouth. My breasts, aching for him, press against his chest as he plants the kiss of a lifetime on me.

He groans as he sinks deeper. And then he pulls back as if he just remembered where we are.

"I told you you'd bring me to my knees before the night was out." He sighs and kisses my forehead. "Goodnight."

And with that, he walks away, down to the waiting car. They wait for me to get inside before they drive away, and I lean on the closed door and take a deep breath.

"He didn't even *try* to come inside," I say to no one. "Not that I would have let him if he did. But he didn't even argue. If I'm so hot in this dress, why didn't he work harder to get me out of it?"

I frown and bite my lip, still tasting him there.

"And why am I mad that he didn't?"

I shake my head and kick out of the shoes that have been killing me all night. I toss my clutch onto the table beside the door and walk to the kitchen for some water.

Callum's flowers sit in my favorite vase on the island.

I sniff them and smile softly.

He's a potent man. But he's a *prince*. And he forgot me once. I won't allow him to do it again.

CHAPTER 6

~CALLUM~

I can still taste her. Feel her spine under my fingertips. I should have controlled myself better, especially at the event. It wouldn't do to have people talking about Aspen, but I couldn't keep my hands to myself.

I feel out of control when I'm with her. And despite a reputation for being reckless, I'm *never* out of control.

But the evening was successful. Aspen enjoyed herself, and once she calmed down about the bloody holiday I bought, she laughed and had fun with the whole group of us.

She fits in well with my family.

I loosen my tie and watch the small town pass by as we drive back to Sebastian's lake house. A few cars are parked downtown, and a handful of people walk on the sidewalks, most likely making their way from pub to pub. Once upon a time, I would have joined them.

But the party life no longer appeals to me. The frivolity of being careless, reckless even, is firmly in my past—and has been for several years.

I'm still restless but in a different way. Ironically, that restlessness seems to subside when I'm in the company of a certain café owner, one Aspen Calhoun.

When we pull into the lake house's driveway, Alice is standing by the path leading down to security headquarters, smiling with excitement.

"Hello, darling," she says to David when we step out of the car. "I was excited to see you and thought I'd meet you here."

"Did you have a nice evening?" David asks his wife before kissing her on the forehead.

"I did. I baked some treats for tomorrow's breakfast."

"Alice, I have a favor to ask," I say, an idea taking shape in my mind. "Would you mind building me a picnic tomorrow? Dinner for two? Well, three if you count this guy." I point to David, who just smirks.

"Of course, I will. I'll have something wonderful ready by midday if that suits?"

"That would be perfect, thank you. Have a good night, you two."

I turn to walk away, but David stops me.

"Callum, I have something for you." He reaches into the car and comes back with a file folder. "Sir, you know I never try to interfere in any way when it comes to the women in your life…"

He swallows hard, and I narrow my eyes, listening.

"However, you need to read this file in its entirety. There are things about Aspen Calhoun that you should know before you pursue her any further. For your sake, and for hers."

He passes me the folder.

"I'll read it tonight," I reply and then pause. "Is she in danger?"

"No, sir," he assures me. "She's safe."

I nod and then walk down the path to the water. I can hear David and Alice walking behind me, but I pay them no mind as I reach the boathouse, key in the code to the door, and climb the stairs to my flat above.

The staff left the light on over the sink. I flip it off and walk in the dark to the bedroom, where I strip out of my suit and exchange it for a white T-shirt and a pair of athletic shorts, then I pad barefoot into the kitchen, fetch a Guinness from the fridge, and carry the folder to the sofa.

I flick on the lamp next to me and open the file. David has organized the information we have on Aspen chronologically by age. Her name then wasn't Calhoun, but Hansen. I skim over school reports and medical records from Tennessee and stop when my eyes see the words *foster care.*

I lean forward, my elbows on my knees as I read through report after report of Aspen being moved between homes until she turned sixteen.

It seems she was emancipated at that tender age and taken out of the system.

What isn't in these reports is emotion. I can't interview anyone or ask questions. I can't ask *why* a child of sixteen was sent off on her own to fend for herself the way an adult would. How did this happen? I regret that Aspen's beginnings started this way, and I wonder what atrocities she endured at the hands of the adults who were supposed to protect her.

I feel the burn of anger simmering in my gut for the young girl who would become such an amazing woman.

I turn the page and blink several times, sure that what I see is wrong.

A death certificate for a Greg Calhoun. And another for Emma Calhoun. Emma was seven. They died five years ago. The cause of death is listed as: *accidental.*

I swallow the bile in my throat and look up from the paper, staring into the darkness.

Aspen was married. She had a child.

I read on in horror as newspaper articles describe in detail what happened to Aspen's family. A tragic boating accident while camping. Search and rescue were called in, and the bodies weren't discovered for two days.

I rub my hand over my face. Jesus, what a bloody mess.

The last piece of paper in the folder is the proof of purchase for Drips & Sips several years ago. It seems

Aspen left Tennessee to start a brand-new life in Montana.

I close the file, set it aside, and reach for my stout. I would rather have heard about this from Aspen herself. Spending late nights in the dark listening to her sweet voice as she tells me about her past. Holding her, consoling her.

But I understand now why David was concerned and wanted me to read it for myself.

First and foremost, it's a warning to tread lightly with Aspen. To be careful.

And to be aware that her past could muddy up any relationship I might choose to pursue with her, at least in the eyes of the press—and potentially my family.

I lean my head back and feel fatigue set in. Aspen's past doesn't put me off in the least. If anything, it only makes her stronger and more resilient in my eyes. I have no intention of backing away.

But I do have questions, and I hope to have them answered very soon.

～

DRIPS & Sips is busy when I walk through the door the next afternoon. I hoped to snatch Aspen away a little early, talk Gretchen into closing for her, but what I find instead is a full café, and Aspen working by herself.

"Hey there," she says when she sees me approach

the counter. I love that she doesn't call me *Your Highness.* She's casual with me. It's a breath of fresh air and just one more thing I enjoy about her. "What can I get for you?"

"I was actually hoping I could steal you away," I reply.

Aspen shakes her head. "Sorry, I can't leave. Gretchen has the day off, and my other helper, Kelli, called out sick. I've been running around like crazy this afternoon."

I immediately turn to David, who's never more than six feet away. "I'm going to help her. The picnic is postponed."

"You're going to *help* her?" he asks.

"Indeed, I am. And you might, as well." I turn back to Aspen. "What do you need us to do?"

"Excuse me?"

"We're at your disposal. What do you need?"

She blows out a breath and checks the time. "Well, we close in thirty minutes. I still have a full dining room. As people leave, I need their tables sanitized, and—"

I walk behind the counter and retrieve the rag she keeps in the bucket, wring it out, and pass it to David.

"We can do that. What else?"

She stares at me like I've gone mad. And maybe I have.

"You don't have to do this. I'm fine. It's not the first

time I've run this show by myself, and it won't be the last."

"But you don't have to," I reply and drag my knuckles down her cheek. "And I admit, I have ulterior motives. I'd like to spend some time with you today. So, just tell me how to help you."

She sighs, and then with a chuckle and a shrug, says, "Okay. Thank you. First…"

Over the next half hour, David and I clear tables, wipe and sanitize, and stock supplies while Aspen cleans her coffee machine. When the last patron leaves, David locks the door and grins at us.

"I have to admit, this was different for us. And most likely against protocol. But it was fun."

"Most people didn't even give us a second glance," I say as I watch Aspen.

"It helps that you dress casually and blend in," Aspen says, glancing our way. "Now, if you were in suits, and if David was packing an AK-47, you'd get some looks."

"I only pack the AK-47 on Tuesdays," David says with a wink. "I'll be right over here when you're ready to go."

He walks over to the far corner of the shop to look out the window and give Aspen and me some privacy.

One of the reasons I love having David on my detail is his discretion.

"I have a plan," I begin and watch as Aspen raises a

brow. "I'd like to take you somewhere special for dinner."

She glances down at her jeans and T-shirt, both a bit of a mess after working all day.

"I'm not dressed for that."

"Actually, for what I have in mind, you're absolutely perfect. Besides, you're gorgeous in anything you wear."

"You're quite charming, aren't you?" she asks.

"Not at all, I'm just being honest. Come with me to a special place for dinner."

She chews her lip but then nods. "You've talked me into it."

"Brilliant."

∽

"Okay, I admit," she says as I lead her down a path toward the river. I can hear the water flowing just past the trees and bushes ahead. "I didn't expect you to bring me up to Glacier National Park for dinner."

"I wouldn't think so," I say with a wink. "Where is that blasted picnic table?"

"It's right over here," she says, pointing to the right.

"You've been here?"

"Of course." Her eyes are full of mischief as she smiles at me. "I come up here about once a week when the weather allows, which is only about four months out of the year."

I want to sigh in defeat, but I just nod and follow her to the picnic table Sebastian told me about. I set our basket on top and take a moment to breathe in the fresh air and look at the beautiful river flowing not ten feet from us.

"Do you have anything this beautiful in Europe?" Aspen asks as she takes a seat at the table and watches the water lazily rushing by.

"Well, yes," I reply. "But it's different. Montana is special; I'll give you that."

"It really is," she says. "What kind of food did you bring? I'm starving."

"Let's have a look, shall we?"

"Do you mean you didn't pack this yourself?" She feigns shock and then giggles. "So, I should give Alice a kiss of gratitude for our meal?"

I narrow my eyes and open the basket, finding a traditional American picnic inside: fried chicken, potato salad, and way more fruit than two people could possibly eat.

David is just a few yards away, also eating dinner. I've told him time and again to join us, especially in moments like these when there isn't anyone else around, but he always insists that it's against protocol.

He loves the word *protocol.*

"This is *so good,*" Aspen says as she takes a bite of her potato salad. "I really will kiss Alice for this."

"I don't love the idea of you kissing anyone, love."

She snorts and takes another bite. "Thank you for

this. I love being up here, and the season is growing shorter by the day. This time next month, we won't be able to get this far into the park."

"It's interesting to me how quickly the weather turns here," I reply.

"On a dime," she agrees. "It's something I had to get used to when I moved here from Tennessee. I lived near the mountains there, so it got chilly in the winter, but nothing like Montana."

"When did you move from Tennessee?" I ask, already knowing the answer but wanting to hear it from her.

She glances at me with a look that says, *really?* "Don't you have a file on me? I'm sure you know this."

I shrug a shoulder. "I'd like to hear it from you."

She looks back at the water.

"A few years ago," she says. "I saw a documentary about the park a few years before that and wanted to see it. One day, I just decided…what the hell? I'll move there."

"And so you did."

"And so, I did," she confirms and takes a deep breath. "Emma would love this."

She frowns as if she didn't mean to say that out loud.

"Tell me about her."

She purses her lips, thinking it over. "They went camping and—"

I stop her. "No, that story is for another time." I lean

in closer and take her hand. "I want to know *about* Emma, not the way she died."

Aspen frowns and tilts her head. "No one's ever asked me that before."

"Shame on them," is all I say as I wait for her to talk.

"She was so funny," she says. "And she had one hell of a temper on her. Of course, she was a redhead like her mama, and we're known for our fire."

"So I've been told," I say, my voice dry as sandpaper. I watch as Aspen laughs.

"She would get this look on her face and puff out her cheeks. Give you major side-eye, even when she was a toddler. When she was super annoyed, she'd give this little growl, which never failed to make me laugh. Of course, that only frustrated her more. She gave me a run for my money, that's for sure. It's a good thing I was so young when I had her, or I would never have been able to keep up with her. She was a whirlwind."

She pauses and pops a piece of watermelon into her mouth, chewing thoughtfully.

"And Emma was no girlie-girl. She wanted to play in the dirt and explore. I couldn't keep the child clean. And her father—" She stops and looks at me. "I'm sorry, you probably don't want to hear about him."

"He is an important part of your life, Aspen. So, yes. I want to hear about him. And anything else you'd like to share about your past."

She swallows hard and glances down at our linked hands.

"I haven't talked much about this in years."

I wait. I'm a patient man.

"Greg and Emma were inseparable," she says. "They loved to play and be outside. She would have lived outside if she could. But with the adventurous spirit came a softer side. She loved to snuggle with me. I used to read to her for hours. Not just at bedtime, but anytime. And she liked to bake cookies with me. Cowboy cookies were her favorite."

"You sell those in the café," I say.

"And I always will. It's honestly a long, sad story, Callum. Longer than I can share in one late afternoon. But there are so many happy memories, too. I miss them both. I don't know if Greg and I would have made it for the long haul. I hate to admit that out loud, especially since the poor man is dead. We married painfully young, and well, who knows what might have happened if they hadn't gone camping that weekend? But he was a good man and a great father. He was my best friend and the one constant I had in my life from the time I was fourteen."

She clears her throat, seemingly determined not to cry.

"Well, this conversation came out of nowhere," she says with a little frown. "But to bring it full circle, Emma would love this spot. She loved picnics, and of course, being outside. She would have asked if we could fish in the river."

I smile and imagine a little girl with Aspen's red hair asking to throw a line into the water.

"Thank you for sharing a little of her with me."

Aspen's green eyes fly to mine. "You're welcome."

"I just have one more very important question about your past, Aspen, and then we'll leave it be for the time being."

Her green eyes look guarded as she waits for the question to come.

"Did you ever have swimming lessons?"

She blinks rapidly. "Of course."

"Good."

I pick her up, sling her over my shoulder, and walk right into the cold water, making Aspen squeal and thrash.

"Callum! Holy shit!"

I squat so she's in the water, and then laugh as she comes up sputtering.

"You're going to pay for that, Charming."

I cock a brow at the nickname. "Oh? And how will I do that, love?"

She launches herself at me, sending me backwards into the water. We swim and splash, laugh and play.

And when we finally trudge our way out of the water and back to the table, I pull Aspen into my arms and kiss her. I don't care that we're both sopping wet and getting a chill from the river.

I need my lips on hers.

And by the way she holds onto my arms as I deepen the kiss, I'd say it's mutual.

When I pull back and smile down at her, her eyes are still closed, and she has a soft smile on her lips.

"Are you okay?" I whisper.

"Yeah," she whispers back. "I'm just soaking it all in."

"The sunshine?"

"The moment. I'm basking in the moment."

CHAPTER 7

~ASPEN~

"Kelli called out again," Gretchen says with a roll of her eyes as she joins me behind the counter. "Seriously, why is it so hard to find good help these days?"

"If I could clone you four times over, I would," I reply with a sigh. "Did she claim to be sick?"

"Yeah, it's a headache this time," she says. "She gives *me* a headache. I won't leave you alone this afternoon. I'll cover it."

"You don't have to do that."

"It's no biggie. Just do me a solid and find someone who actually *wants* to work."

"I'll have a conversation with Kelli, but I have to be careful because there are labor laws." I sigh and watch as a kid walks over to the coffee station where I have sweeteners and self-serve coffee set up, along with creamers and such. I watch in horror as he decides he should pour half and half all over the floor."

"Daniel!" his mother yells, her eyes wide and cheeks pink with embarrassment. "What in the world? Ask Aspen for a rag to clean this up."

"Sowwy," Daniel says. He's not sorry. But I grab a rag and walk around to where he's standing.

"I've got this."

"He should clean it up."

"He's three," I remind Cindy with a shrug and a sympathetic smile. I remember what it's like to have a toddler. "I've got it."

I quickly wipe up the mess. When I turn back around, I see Gretchen looking at her phone with a corny smile on her face.

"Don't tell me."

"I met someone," she says.

"I said, don't tell me."

Gretchen laughs as she tucks her phone back into her pocket. "His name is Miles Johnson. Do you know him?"

I frown, searching my memory. "Doesn't ring a bell. Is he a fireman?"

"No," she says and casually reaches for some tongs to move muffins from one plate to another, consolidating them. "He's actually between jobs, but he says that's because he does construction. He just finished with a house, and they're between projects."

"Hmm." I brew myself a cup of lemon tea.

"He's super hot," Gretchen continues. "And he's totally obsessed with me. I mean, I just met him last Saturday, but we've spent every night together since. He texts me all the time and gets really concerned if I don't reply right away. Like he's worried or something."

Red flags are waving all over the place. "Gretchen, that isn't normal. This is Tuesday. You met him four days ago. There is such a thing as someone being *too* into you."

"I'm needy," she admits with a sigh. I already knew that. "I want a guy who thinks about me nonstop. I *want* him to miss me when we aren't together. I love that he checks in on me and wants to be with me."

I blink at her, watching as a goofy smile spreads over her pretty face.

"He's just so... *sweet.* Like he won't let me make breakfast in the morning. He wants to take me out. Well, I pay, but still, at least he's thinking of me and doesn't want me to overdo it."

"Putting a bagel in the toaster is overdoing it?"

"It's nice not to have to make my own breakfast," she insists and looks down, avoiding my gaze. "It's not expensive."

"Okay, I'm going to say this right here, right now. I don't like this. He sounds like a mooch, and he's glommed onto you, and tells you what you want to hear so he can take advantage of you."

Gretchen clams up and purses her lips. "Or, he really likes me."

"Gretch—"

"Just give me this, okay?" She turns and stares at me with pleading eyes. "Let me have a little fun with a sexy guy. It probably won't go anywhere, but I'm enjoying it for right now."

"Okay." I hold up my hands in surrender. "It's really none of my business anyway."

Just then, the bell over the door chimes, and we get a group of customers, saving me from any more talk about creepy, clingy men. I worry about Gretchen. She so desperately wants to fall in love, and she always tries it with the worst guys possible.

But for the next few hours, there's no time to think about my assistant manager's love life because we're busy with the lunch crowd, and those wanting one more coffee for the afternoon. At one point, all of my tables are full, and we have a line of people waiting for their drinks to go.

I'm grateful Gretchen stayed to help. Working alone this afternoon would have sucked.

"That's the last of them," Gretchen says after the last customers leave. She lets out a gusty sigh. "I'm glad I stayed."

"Me, too. Thanks again."

The bell over the door rings once more, and I half-expect to see Callum since coming at closing time seems to be his modus operandi. Plus, I haven't heard from him in a couple of days. Not that I'm counting. Instead, it's a guy I've never seen before. He grins at Gretchen.

"Hey, sugar," he says.

"Miles!" Gretchen screeches and runs from behind the counter to fling herself into his arms as if she hasn't seen him in years. The kiss that ensues is not just uncomfortable, it's also completely ridiculous.

"You're still on the clock, Gretch."

This does nothing to dissuade them.

"You're fired, Gretch."

Nothing.

"FIRE!"

They jump apart in surprise, and then Gretchen flushes as Miles drapes his arm around her shoulders and tugs her tightly against him.

"I just thought I'd surprise my girlfriend when she got off work."

"She's not off work yet," I reply coolly, watching him with hard eyes.

"But we're done," Gretchen says. "It's only ten minutes early, and I worked an extra shift."

"Yeah," Miles says. "She did you a solid. So we'll be going."

"Hold up." I walk slowly around the counter so I don't slap this piece of crap across his arrogant little face. "This is *my* business, Miles. I call the shots here, not you. From now on, if you're going to meet Gretchen after work, you can either wait in here like a gentleman or stay outside. This little display of…whatever this was won't happen again. Do you understand?"

"So, you work for a bitch, babe," he says, never breaking eye contact with me. "She probably hasn't gotten laid in a while."

"Well, you just made my mind up for me. You can definitely wait outside. Thanks for making it easy. And as for my love life, that's none of your damn business. Gretchen—"

"Miles," Gretchen says, clearly embarrassed. "Aspen's awesome."

"Right. Let's go."

She sends me an apologetic smile and follows the dirtbag out the door.

I let out a long sigh and reach out to flip the lock.

"Oh, Gretchen, this is nothing but trouble."

˜

I HAVEN'T SEEN Callum in a week. Not that I counted on seeing him, it had just suddenly become a habit to run into him every few days. Especially after the picnic in the park and that sexy-as-all-get-out kiss after we played in the water, I thought I might see more of him.

But Callum seems to come and go on his own schedule. I'm grateful that I've been nice to him, and even a little flirty, but not all-in.

Callum isn't the kind of man I can get invested in. He's made that crystal clear. And I'm done feeling angry or bitter about it. He didn't promise me anything. He's *never* promised me anything.

Besides, it could be worse. He could act like Miles, who seems to be stuck to Gretchen like Velcro. I'll take Callum over Miles any day of the week, for several reasons.

I take the groceries out of my car, hurry through the rain to the front door of my house, unlock it, and let myself in. I closed up the café an hour ago, and I'm taking the next two days off.

I can't freaking wait.

I fired Kelli after she admitted that she wasn't really sick but was out on other job interviews. The next day, I hired two college students to replace her. Both of my new hires, Paula and Rachel, are mostly trained, eager for the work, and ready to go. So with Gretchen in charge, they, along with Wendy, my other regular morning help, have it under control.

I'm going to read a book and paint a bathroom. I might even take a nap, which just sounds decadent. If this rain ever clears up, I'll go for a walk.

But the point is, I don't have to do anything at all if I don't want to. I have ice cream in these bags. If I want to loaf around and eat chocolate peanut butter while marathoning the hell out of Netflix, so be it.

I do a little dance in excitement, then turn and

scream when I see a face looking through my back door.

"Sorry!" Callum yells through the glass. He's soaked from the rain, and I hurry over to unlock the door and let him in. "I didn't mean to scare you."

"I have a front door," I remind him as I fetch a towel and pass it to him so he can dry his face and hair. "With a doorbell. When that rings, I don't have a heart attack."

"I saw you go inside with the groceries, and I thought I'd just meet you back here. Bloody bad idea." He dabs at his face and then sets the wet towel on my counter. "Are you okay?"

"As soon as my heart dislodges from my throat and returns to my chest, I will be fine." I take a breath. "I figured you'd gone back to London."

"I did," he admits. "I just returned this morning."

"Oh." I brush my hair out of my face, surprised at this turn of events.

"I had a business meeting that I couldn't miss, and it was better if I appeared in person rather than virtually. I also looked in on my father. I'm not sure if you knew, but he had a heart attack last year, and I don't like being gone longer than a few weeks at a time so I can keep an eye on him."

"I'm sorry, I hadn't heard." I reach out and pat his arm, feeling strong muscles under his long-sleeved shirt.

"It wasn't publicized," he says. "It was a mild heart attack, but it scared the hell out of all of us."

"I'm sure it did. I'm glad he's doing well."

He nods. "All this formality is pissing me off."

Before I can reply, he swoops in and plants his magical lips on mine, kissing me thoroughly. His fingers dive into my hair, and he moans low in his throat as if he's starved for me.

It's intoxicating. Surprising.

Okay, it's pretty damn awesome.

"Did you think I would leave for good and not say goodbye?" he asks, his forehead tipped against mine.

"You did before, and we had sex. And I don't mean that in a bitchy way, I'm just stating the truth."

He frowns. "I really buggered things up with you. Give me your mobile."

"Excuse me?"

"Please give me your mobile."

I comply and watch as he taps the screen, then passes it back to me.

"I added my number in there and texted myself so I have yours, as well. We should have done that years ago. Maybe we could have avoided all that miscommunication."

"You gave me your cell phone number." I blink down at the digits in my phone.

"Yes."

"Like, your private number?"

He drags his knuckle down my cheek. "Indeed."

"Okay, then."

"How have you been?" he asks as he lets me go so I can resume putting away the groceries.

"Busy," I say. "And, honestly, I hate it when people use *busy* as the response to that question. I mean, that's not a good answer. But in this case, that's all I've been. I lost an employee and hired two more, so I had to train them. Gretchen found herself a new boyfriend, which would usually be none of my business, but he's kind of a dick and has decided he likes to hang out in my café when Gretchen's working."

"What's his name?"

My head turns at the steel in Callum's voice. "Why?"

"Because I'm going to have him investigated."

"Oh." I wave him off and shake my head. "He's just a guy who's latched on to Gretchen. But the warning signs are all there that he's a controlling, obsessive jerk, and all she sees is that he's paying attention to her."

"You're worried."

"Of course, I am," I say, folding up my reusable grocery sacks and storing them in the pantry. "She's my employee and my friend, and she's chosen a big jerk to fall in love with. Actually, scratch that. She's not in love at all. She's infatuated, and she has rose-colored glasses on."

"She's an adult," Callum reminds me. "And as frustrating as it is, all you can do is speak your mind. She has to make the decisions for herself."

"She's bad at it," I reply with a sigh. "Enough about me. And her. How are *you*?"

"Frustrated," he says and rubs his hand over his face. "I was called home unexpectedly, and I should have called you to tell you I was going. I missed you while I was away."

"Oh." I smile at the thought of Callum missing me. Maybe Gretchen needs to see that *this* is how missing someone should work. Sure, a phone call would have been nice, but hearing that he thought about me while he was away is wonderful. "I might have given you a passing thought or two over the past week."

His dark eyes narrow. "Just one or two?"

"Maybe three."

He rubs his chin thoughtfully. "Well, I guess that's better than no thoughts at all, isn't it?"

"How long are you in town for? I assume you came to spend more time with Sebastian, Ellie, and the others?"

"I came to town to spend time with *you*," he says. "Yes, it will be nice to see the others, but you're the reason I'm here, Aspen."

I'm not sure what to say.

"What did you think the past few weeks were?" he asks.

"Well, I thought we were being civil with each other because of Ellie."

His eyes flash hot, his temper simmering just below the surface. "I don't kiss women simply to be civil for my baby sister's sake, Aspen. I don't go out of my way to spend time, to get any bloody moment alone I can, so I can try to get to know them better for her. This has absolutely *nothing* to do with Ellie."

"So noted," I say slowly, watching the frustration move over him. "I'm sorry I assumed."

"I'm here because staying away from you isn't a fucking option for me anymore. You're in my dreams. You're constantly in my thoughts. I wonder what you're doing, if you're okay, if you need anything. I picked up the mobile to tell David to get your number for me a dozen times, but I restrained myself because I wanted to see you and talk to you in person.

"So, yes, I flew back across the ocean to spend time with you, not my family."

I swallow hard, my pulse thumping as my blood rushes through my ears. I thought I wanted to hear these things two years ago, but I know now that I wasn't ready for them then.

Am I ready now? Well, if the butterflies in my stomach are to be believed, I'd say yes.

"Can I trust you?" I whisper.

The frustration dims, and regret replaces it. "Yes. And, Aspen, I'm going to say it once again. I deeply regret that I ever lost your trust in the first place. It was never my intent."

I nod and bite my lip. "Well, welcome back to town. Would you like to stay for dinner? I'm making manicotti, and I have enough for two."

He laughs and tugs me to him, wraps his arms around me, and gives me the biggest bear hug ever. I didn't even know that I needed a hug so badly. To be touched and to feel safe in someone's embrace.

In *his* arms.

He gently rocks me back and forth and rubs his hands up and down my back.

"I bet you're a good dancer," I mumble. "I know we danced once before, but I was too busy hating you to admire your dance moves."

"I've had a lesson or two."

"Is it required for the royal family to have dancing skills?" I look up into his face, truly curious.

"It's best if we do, yes. We attend a lot of balls and events where we have to dance. And as much as we hate it, someone is always watching."

"Do you hate being watched?"

He licks his lips and then kisses my forehead. "Being royal isn't something we choose. We were born into this. Which means, we don't choose the media coverage either. It just is. But, yes, it's my least favorite thing about my job."

I'd never considered being a prince a vocation. But it makes perfect sense. I know Ellie is intimately involved with several charities and works tirelessly.

"And how much of what is covered in the media is actually true?" I ask.

"Probably five percent," he replies. "They usually spell my name right."

I laugh. "If I were you, I'd ignore it."

"I do. Unless it's something particularly awful and I

can't avoid it. That hasn't happened in a while, thank goodness."

"So, what kind of work do you do for the royal family?" I ask, just as my stomach growls loudly.

"Why don't you get started on dinner? I'll tell you everything."

CHAPTER 8

~ASPEN~

I pop a bite of crusty bread into my mouth and study the sexy man across from me. Now that we've settled in after the fright of Callum knocking on my back door, and I have some food in my belly, I'm able to concentrate on the conversation at hand.

Callum's more interesting than I originally thought.

"So, you work on behalf of wounded veterans, you're building a special hospital in Edinburgh, and you're part of the British Olympics committee?"

"Among other things, but those are the big ones," he confirms and sips the red wine I opened. "This is delicious, by the way. You're an excellent cook. Where did you learn?"

"My kitchen," I say with a grin, feeling proud of my culinary skills. "When Greg and I were first married, we were dirt-poor. Young, on our own, and struggling to figure life out. There certainly wasn't money for eating out. There was barely enough for groceries. I made it a game. Saw what I could make for five dollars."

"Five dollars per person?"

"For the whole meal," I say, shaking my head. "As it turns out, there's plenty you can make. I just had to be a little inventive. As time went on, and money wasn't quite so tight, I didn't have to be as frugal at the market, but I still enjoyed cooking and playing in the kitchen."

"You could do this professionally if you ever wanted to."

"No." I laugh and take a bite of the pasta. "I'm fine with my café. I do bake a few batches of the cookies sometimes, especially in the winter. Otherwise, I buy everything we have on hand from a local baker."

"Your café is beautiful," he says.

"I love it more than I thought I would," I admit. "I've never been afraid of hard work. But I had no idea that owning a business would be *this* hard. I'm grateful for Gretchen because, even though her taste in men sucks, she's on point when it comes to her job. I can depend on her. And I'm hoping it works out with the new girls so I can take a couple of days off each week. I'm taking this weekend off, and I don't remember the last time I was this excited."

"Is that what you were dancing about when I scared the life out of you at the door?"

I chuckle. "Yes."

"It seems I have good timing for a change, then," he says, studying me over his wine glass. "I have some work to do remotely, but I'd like to spend those two days with you if you'll let me."

I narrow my eyes at him.

"Unless, of course, you have other plans."

"I was going to paint my bathroom and read a book. Maybe take a nap. Obviously, things that can't be rescheduled or juggled."

His lips tip up in a charming grin. "Obviously. If I promise to learn to wield a paintbrush, will you allow me to join you?"

I mentally readjust my plans and grasp onto a new idea. "Actually, I'd like to pick you up in the morning."

He raises a brow. "Where are we going?"

"You'll find out tomorrow."

"So mysterious," he says, slowly shaking his head back and forth, but the humor in his dark eyes is clear. "I'm yours, anytime."

"Eight in the morning," I decide on the spot. "I'd like to sleep in a bit."

"That's sleeping in?"

"I'm usually up at four to open the café at six. So, this will be a treat."

"Eight it is, then. Give me a hint."

"No way."

"A tiny clue."

I laugh and reach for his empty plate to take it to

the sink. "I had a child, Callum. You can try to talk me into it, but it won't work."

"Mums are so strict."

"The good ones are."

"Indeed." I turn to find him watching me. "Did you know your mum, Aspen?"

"Oh, yeah, and she was not a good one," I reply before I can catch myself. I speak about my biological family even less than I do about Emma and Greg. "But that's a boring story."

He just sits and waits. I don't know what it is about this man, but I find myself wanting to confide in him. It's the strangest feeling, and one I don't think I've had before.

"She moved to Nashville to make it big in music. When that didn't work out, she became a junkie. I have no idea who my father is. When I lived with her, I was pretty much on my own anyway. She died when I was five. After that, I bounced around in foster care. I met Greg when I was fourteen, married him the day after I turned seventeen and had Emma later that same year. And, honestly, I wouldn't change any of it."

"Indeed," he murmurs. He's all polish. All slick sophistication.

And I'm just white trash from Tennessee.

What in the hell are we doing?

"Don't even say it," he says, surprising me yet again.

"What was I going to say?"

"That this can't possibly work, whatever this is, because of how different we are."

"Well, would I be wrong if I did?" I ask and lean back against my countertop. Callum stands and slowly walks to me, his gaze never leaving mine. "You're a prince, and I'm—"

"If you say anything other than incredible and the most beautiful, intriguing woman I've ever met, I'll take you over my knee, Aspen Calhoun."

I smile as he saunters closer.

"I can be both intriguing *and* from the wrong side of the tracks, Callum."

"I can't change your past. I'm also not ashamed of it. I'm here because I want to be with you as much as I can. I've wanted that for a long time. But there are some things you need to know."

"I'm all ears."

"My family is openminded and wonderful. The media is not. If you're connected to me, every little detail about your life will be uncovered and examined under a microscope with a lens of disdain, prejudice, and snobbery."

"Did you just say *snobbery?*"

"They will talk about your late husband and the accident that killed both him and your daughter. They'll talk about your childhood. They'll infiltrate your life so completely, you'll feel like a prisoner at times."

"You're really doing a great job of selling yourself here, Your Highness."

His jaw tightens. "You think that your past, where you come from, would make me not want to associate with you. But what *you* need to think about is *my* past and where *I* come from. It isn't always beautiful homes and fancy cars. It's work. It's media. And it isn't private. Never that.

"So what you need to decide between now and tomorrow morning is…do you want to continue this with me? Your history doesn't dissuade me in the least. But mine might discourage you, and I'd rather know that now than after I've finished falling in love with you."

I bite my lip, soaking in every word he said. This isn't to be taken lightly. This isn't something to be viewed through the rose-colored glasses Gretchen wears.

Callum's right, I need to think about this.

Because I'm falling in love with him, too, no matter how much I've tried to convince myself differently.

He leans in and presses his lips to my forehead.

"Thank you for dinner."

"You don't have to go."

He sighs, then kisses me again.

"I do. But I hope I'll see you at eight tomorrow. I'll tell security to expect you."

And with that, he turns and walks out of my house.

I follow to watch through the window. David meets him at the car, and they drive away.

Was David standing out in the rain the entire time? Why didn't I think to ask?

Because it's not normal to have a bodyguard with you everywhere you go.

I keep myself busy with cleaning the kitchen. When that's done, I decide to go ahead and paint that bathroom. No time like the present, right?

∽

I DIDN'T SLEEP IN.

In fact, I didn't sleep much at all.

Because Callum was right. I had to do some serious thinking about what he said. I've seen the media coverage of the royal family. Last year, when Ellie married Liam, the press tore him to shreds because of his military past. They interviewed family that he hadn't seen in years. All my life, the royals were front and center in the tabloids.

And now, because I met a prince absolutely by chance, I could be on the precipice of that same fate.

How in the hell did this even happen?

Oh, yeah, because I thought they might like some scones for breakfast.

I gather my handbag and sunglasses and check the time.

I have to pick Callum up in fifteen minutes.

And, yes, I'm still going.

At about four this morning, I'd almost talked myself out of it. I wanted to keep Greg and Emma's memories safely tucked away, my past forgotten, and move on with my quiet, peaceful life in Montana.

But then I considered never speaking to or seeing Callum again, and the pit in my stomach was unbearable. No, I don't look forward to my past being slung in my face, but I'm not ashamed of it either. I'll stand right up to anyone who wants to say anything shitty about my husband and kid.

And my piece of shit mother wasn't my fault.

I'm a good citizen, with a thriving business in a community I adore. If anyone wants to say anything bad about that, well, let them. I've never been one to give a rat's ass what anyone thinks of me.

Cunningham Falls is quiet this morning, now that the tourists are all gone, and we're back to being a sleepy little town. I roll past Drips, satisfied when I see a short line of regulars at the counter through the window.

When I reach the gate to Sebastian's home, I'm immediately let in and shown where to park.

"His Highness would like for you to meet him at his quarters in the boathouse," a security guard tells me. "I'll be happy to escort you."

"Thank you."

I follow him down the path that leads past the main house, the former guest house that's now the headquarters for security, to the boathouse, where I visited before when Ellie was staying here.

The security guard keys in a code to the door, opens it, and then nods for me to go in.

"Thanks again," I say before climbing the steps to the apartment above. I knock on the door, and almost immediately, Callum opens it. "Good morning."

"You came," he says, his face full of surprise.

"You didn't think I would." It's not a question.

"Honestly, I wouldn't have blamed you if you hadn't. Come in."

He steps back, allowing me to walk into the apartment. I love this space with its open floorplan and expansive views of the lake.

"I almost didn't come. For a couple of hours during the night, I thought of sending you a *thanks, but no thanks* text."

"What changed your mind?" he asks.

"Frankly, I don't care what people say or think about me, Callum. I've had mud slung my way for most of my life. It's not easy to be the poor kid or the pregnant teenager. People talk. As long as you and I are on the same page, that's really all that matters. The rest is just noise."

He frames my face in his hands and plants the newest kiss of the century on me. It's full of relief, joy, and lust.

And when he pulls back to look down at me, his brown eyes are full of gratitude.

"Are you hungry?" I ask.

"Starving."

"I'm taking you out for breakfast."

"Not what I was going for, but that'll work just fine."

I smirk and gesture for him to follow me, but he holds his hands out at his sides.

"Am I dressed appropriately?"

Jeans, T-shirt, Nikes. He looks good enough to eat with a spoon.

"You might want to grab a sweater, but yes. Today is a casual day."

"Brilliant." He tugs a hoodie off a chair and raises a brow when he sees my grin. "What?"

"Royals wear hoodies?"

"And knickers," he confirms with a teasing smile. "Most of the time, at least."

"I definitely won't fit in. I don't wear underwear." I turn to walk down the stairs and hear him mutter, "She's trying to bloody kill me."

Once in the car, I drive us right over to Ed's Diner for breakfast. David agreed to let us drive separately from him, but he's following closely behind. He's going to be a discreet shadow today, which is perfectly fine with me.

"Good girl. You're not taking us to your own business."

"No way. They have it covered there, and I want

greasy food for breakfast. Ed's is the best. Have you been?"

"I don't think so," Callum says as we get out of the car and walk into the diner. We're shown to a red vinyl booth by the windows and given menus. When we're all alone, Callum grins. "This place is fun."

An Elvis song plays on the jukebox. The whole place has an old fashioned Americana feel to it that I just love.

"And Ed himself is manning the griddle back there," I say, gesturing to the kitchen behind the long counter. There's a narrow window Ed passes orders through where he can keep an eye on the dining room. "He's a big, burly teddy bear."

I scan the menu and then set it aside when I make up my mind. After we've ordered, Callum reaches across the table to take my hand.

So it begins. Being seen in public together, clearly not just as friends.

"Someone might take a photo of us," I say quietly.

"You came this morning, love," he reminds me. "I took that to mean you're okay with this."

"I am. I'm just reminding you, in case *you* need to make a phone call to the palace and alert them to all the things that are about to be talked about."

"My family knows I'm seeing you, or that I want to see you. It's one of the things I spoke to them about when I was home last week."

I stare at him in surprise. "You did?"

"Yes. Not to get permission, of course, but to make them aware. Out of courtesy. And that would be the case no matter whom I have in my life, Aspen."

"I understand that. Wow, and here I thought you'd just disappeared again."

"I'm a bloody moron."

I laugh and pat his arm with my free hand. "Nah, you just have to work on your communication skills."

Breakfast is delicious, and before long, we're on our way to our next stop.

"Basically," I say as I drive down Main Street, "I'm taking you to some of the places that made me fall in love with Cunningham Falls. Ed's was the first place I ate when I arrived, and I loved it. We have one pit stop to make before we can resume our tour."

"I'm all yours for the day. Thank you for this."

"You're welcome." I park in front of Brooke's Blooms. "Come on."

I take him inside and buy thirteen sunflowers. I asked Brooke to make sure she had them on hand for me last week.

"These are lovely," Brooke says as she wraps them in brown paper. "If you need anything else, just give me a shout."

"Thanks, Brooke. Have a great day."

"Darling, you shouldn't have," Callum says as we get back into my car.

"Funny. I didn't. I have to deliver these."

His eyes narrow on me, but he doesn't reply as I

drive past Sebastian's house to my special piece of shoreline. I park, take the flowers, and gesture for Callum to follow me.

We walk down to the beach, and I squat as I pull the flowers out of the wrapping and toss one onto the water.

"Today would have been Emma's thirteenth birthday," I murmur as I toss another flower. "So, I brought her thirteen sunflowers. They were her favorite, and they're happy blooms. They remind me of her."

"May I?" Callum holds out his hand for a stalk, and I set it in his palm. He kisses the petals and then sets it on the water. "Happy Birthday, darling girl."

"She would have liked you," I say. "And maybe I should have come here alone earlier this morning, but I didn't have the flowers yet, and—"

"Thank you for allowing me to join you," he says and rubs circles on my back as I toss the final few stems onto the lake. "You should honor Emma on her birthday."

"Thank you." I take a deep breath and let it out slowly. "I come to this spot when I want to do something special for them. They would have liked it here."

"What's not to like?"

"Exactly, it's a beautiful spot." I push up from my squat and feel Callum take my hand, linking our fingers. "Happy Birthday, baby girl."

We're quiet for a long moment. The water is still this morning, and the air is cool, full of autumn.

Just as I'm about to suggest that we go, an eagle soars over the water, then loops around to fly over us. It lets out a loud cry before changing course and heading down the length of the lake.

"Well, it seems she's thinking of you today as well, sweetheart."

I swallow the lump in my throat and lean my head against his arm, feeling the strength of his biceps under my cheek.

"I have so much to show you today. But maybe we can stay here, like this, for just a few more minutes."

"We'll stay as long as you like."

CHAPTER 9

~CALLUM~

She's lovely.

I don't know that I've thought of a woman that way before. Sexy? Yes. Interesting? Sure. Other adjectives might have come to mind when describing other women I've had in my bed.

But I didn't want any of them in my *life*. My world is complicated enough with just me in it, Adding another person didn't seem responsible or appropriate.

Until Aspen.

Now, when I watch the way her green eyes light up when she smiles, or hear the sound of that infectious laugh, or feel her skin against mine, all I can think is: *She's so lovely.*

I'm quite taken with her. My mum would say I fancy her.

And I do.

But it's much more than that. My respect for her as

a woman and business owner has deepened. My appreciation for how she lives her life has strengthened.

And the ferocity with which I crave her has consumed me.

Hearing her speak about her daughter this morning touched me. No one should experience the pain of burying a child. I can't imagine the horror she endured.

And yet, here she is, moving on with her life, and doing it beautifully.

"Do you like ice cream?" she asks as she parks beside a curb.

"Of course." No. I'm not an ice cream fan at all, but if this is what she wants, she'll have it. I'll give her anything her heart desires at the snap of my fingers.

"Good. Because we're going into Sweet Scoops." She grins and then turns to get out of the car. I join her, walking into the small ice cream parlor. We're the only ones in here this afternoon. The weather has been moody all day, vacillating between pleasant and torrential rain.

"Hi, Aspen," the woman behind the counter says with a smile. "I didn't see you at the chamber of commerce meeting last week."

"Hey, Lydia. I know, I had a hell of a week. I'll make the next one. This is Callum."

Shrewd eyes turn to me. Of course, she recognized me the minute we walked in, but the thing about Cunningham Falls is that no one seems to acknowledge the royals' presence.

"Hello, Lydia," I say with a nod.

"Nice to meet you," Lydia replies. "What can I get you two?"

"I'll have a scoop of the huckleberry, of course," Aspen says, then turns to me expectantly.

"The same, please."

"Two hucks, coming up," Lydia says and gets to work scooping the ice cream into cups. She passes them over, along with plastic spoons, and we go to sit at a table to enjoy the treat.

"So, we've been to Frontier Park," I say, thinking about our day so far. "Ed's Diner. Drove around the entirety of the lake, went to the birds of prey sanctuary where I fed baby owls, and now we're having ice cream."

"Busy day," she says with a nod. "There are some other places I could take you, but they're a bit of a drive away, and I'm getting tired. This will probably ruin my dinner, by the way."

"Who says ice cream can't be dinner?"

Her green eyes warm, and she grins as she licks some ice cream from her spoon.

Jesus, the image that just went through my brain of her using that tongue elsewhere should be illegal.

"What's your favorite ice cream flavor?" she asks.

"Actually, I have a confession." I sigh and take the last bite, then set the cup aside. "I don't love it at all."

Her eyes go wide. "You should have said so!"

"No. You're showing me what *you* love about this

town, and this is a piece of that. I'm not a sweets person. But give me a bag of crisps, and I'll eat the whole thing."

"What's your favorite kind of *crisp?*" she asks.

"I'm quite fond of the American barbeque ones," I reply. "What's next on our agenda?"

"I have one last place to take you." She stands, and I join her, walking behind her to the door. She loses her grip on her handbag, and it falls to the floor. When she reaches down to retrieve it, her jeans rip, right down the crack of her arse.

She stops cold, then straightens, and I quickly move in to stand directly behind her as I take off my jumper and wrap it around her waist.

"Well, well," I say into her ear, unable to keep the humor out of my voice as my cock stirs in my trousers. "You weren't lying when you said you don't wear knickers."

She blows out a breath of disgust.

"It's the manicotti," she says. "I ate so much, my ass grew two sizes. I can't believe that happened, especially in front of *you.*"

"Better in front of me than in front of some other bloke I'd have to tear into shreds for looking at your fine arse." I pull my lips away from her ear and finish tying the jumper's arms around her waist. "That should get you home."

"Thank you." She leads me out to her car. David's brows climb when he sees my clothes wrapped around

Aspen. She shrugs at him. "Change of plans, David. We're headed back to my house."

"Yes, miss." He nods and follows us back to Aspen's house. She hurries up the front steps, lets us inside, and turns to me.

"Make yourself at home. I'm just going to run and change my pants. It's a bit drafty running around like this."

I laugh and watch as she unties the jumper and tosses it to me, then turns and walks out of the room, her bare arse exposed.

I rub my hands over my face. Jesus, I want her. I've never wanted anyone the way I do Aspen Calhoun.

Rather than stomp down the hall behind her, toss her onto the bed, and have my wicked way with her, I look around her home. She has excellent taste in art and furniture. I wander down the wide hallway, admiring the artwork on the walls, and turn into her bedroom.

There isn't just a splash of color. Color and texture are everywhere. Rich, red bedding, pillows in greens and purples, some in satin, and others in velvet. The furniture is simple but sophisticated.

This room reflects what I know about Aspen. Sexy. Fun. Classy. I can see us tangled in those sheets, moving together, exploring each other.

A photo on the side table catches my eye, and I immediately reach for it.

It's Aspen with a little girl, who I assume is Emma. They're smiling at the camera, holding up teacups.

"We were at a tearoom in Nashville," she says. I look up to find her leaning on the doorjamb, her arms crossed over her chest, looking at the photo in my hands. "She *loved* tea parties. It was the only girlie thing she enjoyed, and it was something we did together all the time. So, when she got to be old enough to appreciate being there, I made us a reservation at this gorgeous tearoom. She was enthralled with the owner's accent, and after the day that photo was taken, she mimicked it when we had our tea parties at home."

"That's quite adorable."

"It was a happy day, so I've kept the memory by the bed."

I nod and set the photo down, then turn to the woman who's captured my attention so completely.

"I ruined a perfectly good pair of expensive jeans," she says with a sigh, but her eyes are full of humor. It seems that talking about Emma doesn't leave her sad at all. She tips her head to the side. "What are you thinking?"

"That I love how easily you speak of your daughter, and that it doesn't leave you distraught."

"I don't speak of her often, to be honest. But, no. It used to make me very sad. And I still miss her. But I read a quote once, and it resonated with me. '*If you don't heal from what hurt you, you'll bleed on those who didn't cut you.'* I don't know who said it, but I've thought about tattooing it on my body."

"Why don't you?"

"I haven't had the time," she says with a small smile. "Have I ever told you that I like your ink?"

"No. In fact, until very recently, you made it a point to make sure I knew that you didn't like *anything* about me."

"Well, my pride was bruised," she says with a shrug. "And I'm done bleeding on you."

"I'm the one who cut you."

"I healed." She pushes away from the doorway and walks to me. "I was surprised the day I saw the tattoos on your arm. You're the bad boy prince, aren't you?"

"I'm not a direct heir to the throne," I reply and have to swallow hard when she drags her fingertips up the arm in question, currently covered by my long-sleeved shirt. "And I do cover them when I'm in an official setting, out of respect. But my body is my own."

"Is that why you didn't finish the sleeve all the way to your wrist? So it's easy to cover?"

"That's right."

I can smell the citrus in her hair as Aspen raises her gaze to mine. You could cut the sexual tension in this room with a bloody knife.

"Are you ever going to kiss me?" she asks. Her voice is rough, her eyes pinned to my lips.

"Hell, yes." I'd be a bloody idiot to make her ask again. I swoop in and cover her mouth with mine, drinking her in. Her hands dive into my hair, and she holds on tightly, giving me as good as I give.

I want to tear her clothes off and have my way with her. I remember, in great detail, what it feels like to be buried deep inside her, where I don't know where I end, and she begins. To be consumed by her.

I spin her around and guide her back to the bed. I need a taste of her.

I push her T-shirt up her belly and nibble the soft, smooth flesh revealed, delighted when goosebumps break out over her skin.

"You're so damn responsive," I mutter and move up between her breasts. I fucking love the way she feels beneath me. The way she smells.

Every bloody thing.

But I'm just starting to gain her trust back, and I won't take the chance of ruining everything now—because I plan to have Aspen in my life for a *very* long time.

For the first time in my life, I can see myself married, perhaps with children.

And I want it with Aspen.

I nibble a bit on her neck and then settle in to kiss her softly, slowing things down. Her lips are soft, plump, and wet. She's every dream I've ever had.

I place a kiss on the tip of her nose and lean back to smile down at her.

"Why did you stop?" she asks.

"Because we have time." I link our fingers and kiss

her hand. "I'm not here just for sex. We'll get there. I want much more than that with you, and I don't want you to think that I'll bed you and leave you again."

"*Bed* me?" She snorts. "You didn't *bed* me the first time."

She laughs, an all-encompassing belly laugh this time, and I can't help but join her.

"Bed me," she says after she takes a deep breath. "That's hilarious. This isn't 1677, Your Highness."

"You know what I mean."

"You're not going to fuck me and forget me again." There's no anger in her voice, but I wince. Having that tossed in my face will likely always sting.

"No. I'm not." And hearing the words crassly spoken in that way angers me. I sit on the side of the bed and push my hands through my hair in agitation. "And one of these days, you'll finally believe me."

"I believe you today," she says, sitting next to me. "If I didn't, I wouldn't have been ready to get naked just now."

I cup her cheek. "We're getting there."

"I'll cook you dinner," she offers. "I was thinking of putting together some chef salads."

"I think I'll call it a day," I reply and soften the rejection with a deep kiss. "I have a couple of calls to make before London goes to bed. I'd like to see you tomorrow, though."

"I'm available all day."

"Make no mistake," I say when I see the confusion

in her gorgeous eyes, "when you're ready, I'll take us both to bed for days, surfacing only for food. I want you more than I want my next breath, but I have to make sure we're on the same page, Aspen. It's imperative."

"Why?"

"Because you matter. This matters. At that's why I'm treading carefully."

She blows out a gusty breath. "Well, how am I supposed to argue with that?"

"You can't."

∽

She brought me BBQ crisps. Not just one kind. Or two. But *three* bags of my favorite snack.

I've already blown through one as we lounged around my flat all day, watching movies. I tried to get her to watch European football with me, but after fifteen minutes, she started to fall asleep, so we changed things up.

"I love that you're here with me today," I say as I pull her legs up onto my lap and press my thumb into the arch of her foot.

She moans beautifully, making my cock stir.

"But if you have other things to tend to on your last day off, I understand."

"If you stop rubbing my foot, I might scream. If you

wanted me to leave, you should have said so before you started doing that."

"I don't want you to leave. I was trying to be thoughtful."

Her plump lips tip up into a grin. "I'm doing exactly what I want to be doing on my day off."

"Good, because I was going to hold you hostage anyway. Please don't make me watch another sappy romantic comedy this afternoon, love."

"What would you rather watch? Besides soccer."

"It's football."

"It's soccer."

"We could watch a Bond film," I suggest.

"That'll make me nap for sure," she replies. "What about a documentary on serial killers?"

I stop rubbing and frown at her. "Seriously?"

"Yeah. I like them."

"I knew I liked you." I reach for the remote and flip on Netflix, paging through the options until I find what we're after. "Before I start this, should we get dinner?"

"I don't want to go anywhere."

"We can get takeaway," I suggest. "I can ask someone to fetch us pretty much anything your heart desires."

"How can you be hungry after eating that whole bag of chips?"

"David and I ran for fifteen miles this morning."

Her eyebrows climb in surprise, and I raise her big toe to my lips and press a kiss to the pad of the digit.

"You'll be burning calories for days," she replies. "I think I want a burger from Ed's. With onion rings and a shake."

"That's Ellie's favorite, as well," I reply. "And that sounds delicious to me. Let's get takeaway, eat too many calories, and watch this macabre documentary all evening. Shall we?"

"Oh, we shall. We shall indeed." Her nose is in the air as she tries to mimic my accent.

She's so bloody adorable.

In less than an hour, we're seated on the floor with our meal spread out before us on the coffee table, and the show queued up on the tele.

"I think you already know this about me, but before I dig into all of this deliciousness, you should know that I'm not one of those girls who picks at her food. I *eat*."

"Good. Eat."

She shoves her burger into her mouth and takes a massive bite before sighing in delight. When our stomachs are full, we move to the sofa, and I pull Aspen into my arms. We're dressed in sweats and socks, our legs tangled. I kiss the top of her head and breathe her in.

"This is lovely," I whisper.

"The fact that two women have been raped and beheaded so far in this episode?" she asks.

I chuckle. "No. Being here. With you, like this. Holding you. It's quite nice."

"I agree." She kisses my cheek and then points at the screen. "Don't do it! Don't marry him. You're asking for trouble."

"I hope that's not your typical advice to women who wish to wed."

"Nah, I keep those opinions to myself."

"You were married once."

"Once," she agrees. "And I most likely won't be again."

My heart stills. "No children either?"

"I don't think so," she replies. "I've done those things, and it didn't work out for me. I'm not in a hurry to try it again. Although, one thing I've learned is to never say never."

I want those things with her. Desperately. And I plan to have them. But for tonight, I'm content to have Aspen in my arms, here like this, where the rest of the world isn't watching, and we can simply be together. The idea of not being with this woman for the rest of my life is out of the question.

"Stay tonight," I whisper in her ear. "Just let me hold you. Nothing more."

"I have to be at Drips early in the morning," she replies.

"I'll get up with you," I promise. "I'd like to have you with me tonight. I told you, it won't go further until you're ready, and we're getting there. But this is too lovely for me to say goodbye this evening."

"I'd like to stay," she says.

"Thank you."

∽

"Hello, Mum." I press the mobile to my ear and watch the lake reflect the moonlight. It's getting dark earlier each day as we move toward winter.

"How are you, darling?" she asks. I can hear the smile in her voice. My mum is simply the best there is. One minute, she can be the consummate queen, foreboding and regal. And the next, she's laughing and playing with her children or grandchildren.

We all adore her.

"I'm doing well. And you?"

"Just lovely, thank you. How are things in Montana? Your father and I must get over there to see this place that has captured our children's attention so. The photos are beautiful."

"They don't do it justice." I take a sip of the whiskey I poured when I walked into the flat after having dinner with my family. I haven't seen Aspen since she left for work this morning, and I needed the distraction. "You'd enjoy it very much. I hope you'll come to visit soon."

"It's never a good idea to have so many members of the family gone at once," she reminds me.

"Frederick never leaves Europe," I say. "The commonwealth will be just fine if you and Father take a holiday in the States for a few weeks."

"I suppose you're right. I'll have a chat with your father. What's on your mind, Callum? I know you didn't call to simply talk about holidays."

"I suppose not." I drain the rest of the glass. "I'd like to talk about Aspen."

"Have you been seeing her?"

"Yes."

"And?"

"I'm in love with her."

She's quiet for a moment. "I knew that when you stood here in the palace last week and told us about her. I've never seen that look on your face before."

"And how big is the shit storm going to be when I ask her to marry me?"

"*Callum.*" I can just picture her jaw dropped in surprise. "You *are* in love with her. Well, I knew that when it happened for you, it would be all-encompassing. You're not one to give emotion away frivolously."

"No. I'm not."

"We read the report from security on her past," she says slowly. "I assume you did the same?"

"Yes, and I spoke with her about it at length. I also suggested that she think long and hard about being with me because this life is no picnic."

"And what did she say?"

"That she's not ashamed of her past or the events

that led her to where she is now. And that us being of the same mind is the most important thing."

"I think I'm going to like this woman very much."

"You will. But, Mum—"

"Your father and I are traditional people," she says, interrupting me. "We take our duties seriously and love our family's history. But we're also not going to tell you that you can't follow your heart. We learned valuable lessons with both Sebastian and Ellie in that regard. And now, both of them are happily married to the people meant for them."

"I need you to do me a favor, Mum."

"Anything, you know that."

"It's not a small thing."

"It never is with you, darling."

I smile with the knowledge that she's not being cold but telling the truth.

I've never been easy.

I outline my idea to Mum, and by the time I hang up, we have a plan in place—as long as my father agrees.

The king always has the final say.

I would have spoken to him this evening, but he was already asleep.

The clouds from the past few days have cleared, leaving the sky scattered with millions of stars. It's amazing how clear the sky is here. How quiet the nights.

I walk back inside, ready to open my laptop and

work for a few hours before I try to sleep when I hear a knock at my door.

I frown. Usually, if David or any of the others need me, they text or call.

I cross to the door and open it, shocked to find Aspen standing on the other side of the threshold with wide green eyes, slightly out of breath as if she ran all the way from her house.

"Security told me you'd cleared me to come whenever, but if you'd rather I call—"

"You're welcome here. Any time, day or night, Aspen."

She swallows and nods twice. She looks nervous.

Christ, is she going to tell me it's over? What in the hell has happened over the last twelve hours?

"Callum, I'm ready."

I narrow my eyes. "Ready for what?"

She raises a brow, and I suddenly know down to my bone marrow what, exactly she's ready for.

"I'm *ready*."

"Are you sure?"

"I've never been more sure about anything in my life."

CHAPTER 10

~ASPEN~

*J*esus, I've never been so nervous in my life. I'm out of breath, my mind is racing, and if Callum turns me away, I'll die of humiliation.

I might anyway.

But he tugs on my hand and pulls me into the apartment. Rather than strip me bare and carry me into the bedroom the way I pictured it in my head on the way over here, he calmly takes my jacket off, tosses it over a chair, and leads me into the living area.

"Have a seat. Would you like some wine? Whiskey?"

"No, thank you. You don't have to get me drunk to have sex with me, Callum."

He rubs his hand over his mouth and sits in the chair opposite me, his elbows braced on his knees as he watches me with those dark eyes.

"If you'd rather I go…" I stand to leave, but his calm, deep voice interrupts me.

"Sit down, Aspen."

I comply.

"I don't want you to go. In fact, it's lovely to see you. I was just thinking about you."

"You don't seem happy to see me." I don't like the vulnerability in my voice. I've been so used to keeping my walls up with this man for so damn long, letting them down isn't easy. But I can't stop it. I've fallen in love with him, and if that means I end up with a broken heart, then so be it.

"You took me by surprise, that's all." He reaches out for me and tugs me into his lap. He brushes the tip of his nose against my cheek. "Seeing you is always a punch in the stomach."

I lean back to look into his eyes. "Why?"

"You're so bloody beautiful. With this amazing red hair that just begs for my hands, and big green eyes that seem to see right through me, even when I don't want them to. You take my breath away."

"You're so good with the pretty words."

"They're not just pretty, they're true. If you came here tonight, it tells me that you were thinking of me, as well."

I brush my finger down his chin, enjoying the feel of his stubble. "I think of you often, Callum. It used to infuriate me."

His lips twitch.

"And now?"

"I'm not angry. I'm not even confused. And I'm not the kind of woman to play coy games or beat around the bush, so I'll just say what's on my mind."

"By all means, please do."

"When you're here, it's like the missing piece of a puzzle is finally in place. And when you're gone, there's a hole where you were. I don't know if that makes sense."

"Makes perfect sense to me." He kisses my temple as his hands start to roam over my body, stirring my blood and my libido.

"I know we're different, and I'm lost as to how something between us can work, but I also don't want to stop seeing you."

"One day at a time is a perfectly reasonable plan in moments like these." He kisses that sensitive area behind my ear, and I feel him harden against my hip.

Before he can make a move, I slip off his lap and kneel between his legs. I drag my hands from his chest, down his flat and ridiculously muscled belly to the waistband of his slacks.

His brown eyes shine in the low light as he silently watches me pull the button free, then unzip them and reach inside to pull out his cock.

"Bloody hell," he mutters.

"I've been thinking about this for a long time," I whisper before I lean in and lick around the crown of his hard cock. When I sink down, pulling a good portion of his length into my mouth, and then tighten my lips and pull back up again, he moans and threads his hands into my hair.

"You *are* trying to kill me."

I hum around him and repeat the motions over and over again, sinking down, tightening my lips, and pulling back up. All the while, I work him with my hand. When I feel his balls tighten and lift, Callum grabs my shoulders and forces me to stop.

"Aspen, coming in your mouth sounds like heaven, but I haven't been inside of you in two years, two months, and six days, so we're going to take a raincheck on that incredible offer and set it aside for today."

"You know exactly how long it's been?"

"I didn't mention the six hours and forty-ish minutes." He guides me to my feet and kisses me hard before leading me to his bedroom.

"I want the lights on," I say, surprising him. "Unless someone can see in here."

"I'll close the shutters." He makes quick work of it, and when he turns back to me, I'm already naked, waiting for him. "I don't know what I did right in this life to deserve this, but I'll do it every fucking day if this is my reward."

I smirk and crook my finger at him, encouraging him to *come here*.

"Why do you want the lights on, Aspen?"

"Because I want to see you. Your body, your ink,

your eyes when you look at me and when you're about to lose your shit. I want to see it all."

His skin is tanned and smooth over muscles that go on for weeks. That ink on his arm begs for my tongue. And his cock is hard and proud, just waiting for me.

"Same page, darling."

He doesn't reach for me yet. Instead, he jerks his shirt over his head and lets it fall to the floor. He drops his slacks, sending them with his shirt, and I can't wait to get my hands on him.

I'm freaking *salivating*.

"You're something to look at yourself, Your Highness."

"Callum," he corrects me and steps forward. "When we're here, like this, I'm not a prince or Your Highness. I'm Callum, or Cal if you like. Because our jobs and our families have no place here. This is you and me."

"Anything else I need to know before I destroy you for all other women?"

His lips tip up in a smug, satisfied smile.

"Darling, you already have."

He slowly moves toward me, and just when I think I might die from anticipation, his fingertip circles my nipple, making it pebble. He leans over and plucks it into his mouth, then lets go with a loud *pop*.

The cool air is almost painful on the sensitive skin, but before I can say or do anything in response, Callum's hand glides down my hip, my thigh, and back up to my core.

"So wet."

"Entirely your fault."

"Oh, I'll happily take the blame." His finger pushes inside me, and I groan in pleasure. "I'm going to make you scream my name before the night is out."

"Promises, promises."

My knees are shaking, but before my legs can fail me, Callum lifts me and carries me to the bed, laying me in the center of the big King-sized mattress. The bedding is soft, and this man is better than I remember.

And we haven't done much yet.

He parts my legs and settles between them, his dick resting against my folds, but not entering me as he leans in to kiss me. His fingers are in my hair, and his hips rock back and forth through my slickness.

"I know we have time," I whisper between kisses, "but *hurry up*."

"You're so impatient."

"Yes." I don't even try to deny it. I reach between us, cup him, and guide him to my center, but he suddenly curses against my lips.

"Condom." He reaches into the bedside table and retrieves the protection. Seconds later, he's nudging his way inside of me. "Holy fuck."

"Mm."

He lifts my legs and sits back so we can both watch as he moves in and out of me. He presses the pad of his thumb against my clit, and I see stars. He nibbles on the arch of my foot, and it's game over. My pussy contracts, my back arches, and I come harder than I ever have in my life.

When I open my eyes, Callum's still moving slowly, kissing my leg as he watches me.

"Wow."

"Round two," he says and pulls out long enough to flip me onto my tummy. He presses my legs together, spreads the cheeks of my ass with his thumbs, and enters me again, making me call out. The change in position is earth-shattering. His thumb rubbing my lips as he fucks me is *everything.*

"Callum."

"Louder."

I can't speak. I can't even *think.* My body is in overdrive as he pounds into me, over and over.

He grips my hair at the nape of my neck and pulls, just enough to make me groan.

"I said louder."

"I can't."

He spanks my ass and fucks me even harder, and the orgasm consumes me. As I fall over the edge, I cry out, *"Callum!"*

"That's fucking right."

He pushes and then jerks, succumbing to his own orgasm, and then he rolls off me, collapses next to me, and we spend the next five minutes simply trying to breathe.

"I need a ventilator," I say at last and push my hair

out of my face so I can look at my handsome prince. "Do you have one handy?"

"I can't say that I do." He turns his head and smiles at me. "But if you find one, I could use it, too."

"I don't even know if I still have legs."

"You do, and they're sexy."

"Oh good."

"Can I get you anything, love?"

"Water."

"I have a shower full." To my amazement, he stands and tugs me out of bed and then tosses me over his shoulder as he makes a beeline for the bathroom.

"I haven't even caught my breath."

"You can do that while I wash your back."

~

"I'm starving."

I'm lying on Callum's chest, brushing my fingers through the very light spattering of hair there, listening to my stomach growl.

"Twelve hours of sex will do that to a person," he says.

"You're smug."

"You're bloody right, I am. I've been waiting a long time for last night." He kisses my hand and then holds it against his heart. "Two years without sex is a frustratingly long time, darling."

My head pops up, and I stare at him as if he just told me he's Mickey Mouse.

"Are you telling me that—?"

"You ruined me for all other women. At least, I think that's how you phrased it last night. And if you go into a long list of men you've been with since our time together, I may turn homicidal, so let's not."

"Oh, please." I laugh and bite his chest, just for fun. "I've been with exactly *two* men in my life, and I'm lying on one of them right now."

He rolls me onto my back and stares down at me intently. "You hadn't been with anyone but your husband when I met you?"

"No."

"And you haven't been with anyone since?"

"Keep rubbing it in."

He drags his knuckles down my cheek. "No wonder you wanted to kill me."

"Murder crossed my mind a time or two." I stretch under him, fully aware that my breasts are on display for him. "But I'm glad you're still alive."

He drags his nose over my tight nipple and then sighs.

"No more apologies," I say before he can offer the words. "We're in a good place now. Let's not rehash old news, okay?"

"Deal." He plants a kiss on me, then leaves me altogether. "Put on some clothes. We'll go up to the main house for breakfast. Alice most likely has something delicious cooking, and I don't keep much food here."

"You want me to go up to see your family, dressed in last night's clothes, after we spent the night having sex?"

He blinks down at me. "What's wrong with that scenario?"

I shrug a shoulder. "It kind of screams *walk of shame*, but okay."

"Actually, it says I had a nice evening with you, and I'm not ashamed in the least."

I know that the grin spreading over my face is goofy, but I don't care. "Okay, let's go get breakfast."

"Excellent."

I tug on the jeans and T-shirt I wore last night, use my fingers on my hair to try and make it presentable, but end up throwing it up into a knot instead. Then I root around under the sink in the bathroom for a new toothbrush.

Which I find because Nina and her staff always think ahead.

Once I've brushed my teeth and am ready to go, Callum escorts me from the boathouse to the primary residence, which is bigger than any other house I've ever been in. With massive windows that face the lake and enough space for the population of all of Montana, it's a dream home.

I follow Callum up to the main living space, which includes a huge, open kitchen and sitting room with the same impressive views of the water that the boathouse has.

Thank God Callum's bedroom doesn't face the house.

"Good morning," Nina says with a smile. She and Sebastian are sitting on a couch, cuddling, while Alice bustles about in the kitchen. "And welcome."

"Thank you."

I've met Nina and her husband Sebastian several times, and they've always been kind to me.

"Hello, Aspen," Alice says with a wave. "How lovely to have you here. I hope you enjoy crepes and muffins."

"What's not to enjoy?" I ask, just as Ellie and Liam come walking through the front door.

"Good morning," Ellie says, and then her face lights up when she sees me. "What a wonderful surprise. How are you, Aspen?"

"I'm great, thank you. You guys, please forgive me, but am I supposed to curtsey or something?"

Everyone laughs, but Ellie shakes her head. "No, silly. This is as informal as it gets. We're family, and friends."

"Please just give me a heads-up if I botch something, okay? I can learn. I'm not completely clueless."

"I was when I met him," Nina says, gesturing to Sebastian. "I had to learn from scratch, and let me tell you, there was a lot to learn. But you'll catch on. As long as we're in a casual situation like this, you can just act normally."

"Thank you."

Callum kisses my cheek and then gestures for me to have a seat with the others.

"So, things are going well, then?" Ellie asks and elbows Liam. "I told you it would go well."

"I had no idea you were such a matchmaker," I say as I accept a cup of coffee from Alice. "Thank you so much."

"You're welcome."

"I'm not usually, I just had a feeling, and gave you a little push."

"I didn't need a push," Callum says while pouring cream into his coffee. "And you can mind your own business, baby sister."

"Where's the fun in that?"

"All right, everyone, everything is ready for you. Would you rather I serve you in there, or would you like to eat buffet-style?"

"No need to serve me," Sebastian says. "We'll come make our own plates, Alice. Thank you."

"Of course." Alice nods and turns away, but stops suddenly and presses her hand to her head. "Oh, my."

"Alice?" Nina says, just as the woman falls to the floor unconscious.

"Go get David," Sebastian says to Liam, who's already running for the door. Callum has Alice's head in his lap and is feeling for a pulse. "Is she alive?"

"Yes, it looks like she passed out," Callum says as

Alice starts to come to. David and Liam run into the room.

"What's going on?"

"She fainted," I say. "Should I call for an ambulance?"

"Give me a second," David says, kneeling beside his wife and taking her in his arms. "What's happened, sweetheart? Are you okay?"

"I just got so lightheaded," she says and shakes her head. "I passed right out. But I think I'm fine now."

"You should see a doctor," Sebastian says. "We can get one here today."

"I'll call Hannah," Nina says as she reaches for her mobile. "She'll come right over."

"Hannah is her friend, who happens to be a gynecologist," Ellie tells Alice.

"Really, there's no need to fuss. I'm fine."

But Nina is already speaking to Hannah, who promises to come right over.

"She lives about ten minutes away. She'll be here soon."

"I think we're making a big deal out of this," Alice insists.

"I don't," David says. "Let her have a look and make sure there's nothing wrong."

Callum slips his hand into mine and gives it a squeeze. I love being here, among these people who clearly care deeply for one another. The royal family values their employees and treats them like family.

That says a lot about them, and the people they come from.

Hannah arrives within minutes, carrying a bag and a stethoscope around her neck.

"I know you don't usually make house calls," Nina says, "so thank you for this."

"Not a problem at all. I'll just take some vitals." She approaches Alice with a smile. "How are you feeling now, Alice?"

"Foolish," the other woman says. "I'm sorry to waste your time."

"Helping friends is never a waste," Hannah says and takes Alice's temperature. "Why don't we go somewhere more private?"

"Of course, there's a guest room right through here," Nina says, escorting the other two women, and David, away.

"Well, this is a busy morning," Sebastian says while he digs into his crepe. The rest of us follow suit, filling the time until we hear how Alice is doing.

"That woman can *cook*," I announce after the first bite. "If she didn't already work for you, I'd hire her in a heartbeat."

"She's quite talented," Callum agrees. "And inventive. She talked our father into eating things that I never thought I'd see."

"Father is a picky eater," Ellie adds.

Finally, after we've all eaten our fill of breakfast, the other women return to the room.

"Thank you again, Hannah," Alice says, shaking her hand. "I'll come see you next week."

"Perfect. Have a great day, everyone. I have to get to the office."

With a wave, Hannah leaves, and we're all left staring at Alice and David, who both have goofy grins on their faces.

Before they say anything at all, I know.

"Well?" Callum asks.

"I'm going to have a baby," Alice replies and is swept up in hugs and well wishes.

"It's a good day," I say as I lean my head on Callum's shoulder. "A very good day."

CHAPTER 11

~ASPEN~

These past couple of weeks have been like living in a fairy tale, and I stopped believing in those many moons ago. If I ever did at all.

I'm dating a prince. Like, an honest to God prince, not just someone named Prince. And I'm still not sure how that happened, but I don't want it to stop anytime soon.

We haven't spent a night apart in two weeks. Mostly, I stay at the boathouse at night because David should be with his wife. It's just easier, security-wise. And I like the boathouse. There's really no need for me to be home, especially now that we're firmly into autumn, and my summer duties around my property are all over for the season. Meaning, no watering, weeding, or pulling vegetables out of the ground. So, spending time away isn't hurting anything.

And I don't know how long this will last, how long

Callum will be here, so I'm soaking in every minute I can.

Callum is romantic, attentive, and funny. He's also damn good at his job. This morning before I left for work at the ass crack of dawn, Callum was already up and arguing over the phone about something to do with the Olympic committee.

The other person on the line finally saw things Callum's way. I have a feeling they usually do.

Hearing his stern voice was a turn on. I didn't know before him that I had a thing for gruff, *intense* men. And I don't outside of the bedroom.

But when we're in bed? Holy hell, his intensity, the way he takes control with a firm hand renders me defenseless in the best way possible. A shrink would probably tell me it's because nobody's done that for me in any context over the course of my life. I've always had to make the decisions and fend for myself. Being with a man who takes the reins out of my hands, at least where intimacy is concerned, is liberating.

And they'd be right.

But I'm also leaning toward *it's hot as fuck.*

I smirk at the thought as I put the tray of fresh huckleberry muffins into the display case. We're about fifteen minutes from opening, and so far, I haven't seen or heard from Gretchen.

In the past, that was unusual. Since she's been seeing the douche nozzle, sadly, it's the norm.

I hate that guy.

The door dings and, speak of the devil, there's Gretchen and the boyfriend of the year himself.

"Good morning," Gretchen says. Her eyes look tired, but she offers me a small smile.

"Hello." My eyes turn to Miles. I don't smile. "Miles."

"Hey there, boss lady," he says with a wink. "Don't worry, I'm not here to stir up any trouble, I'm just dropping off my girl for work. I'd love to take a cup of coffee with me."

"That'll be three-fifty." I pass him the empty cup so he can fill it himself at the self-serve station.

"No employee discount?" he asks.

"You're not now, nor will you ever be, my employee." I'd rather go out of business.

"Ouch." He winces and then shrugs as he passes me a five-dollar bill. "Give the change to Gretch, will ya?"

I roll my eyes and turn to the cash register. Miles takes his time making his coffee, then turns with a wave for Gretchen. "Have a good day, hon. I'll see you this afternoon."

"Bye," Gretchen calls after him. When the door closes behind his sorry ass, I turn to my employee.

"Why are you still seeing him?"

"Don't start, Aspen," she says with a sigh. "I know you don't like him, but I do."

"Why do you look so tired?"

"Because I was up late and had to work early this

morning." She presses her lips together, and it's clear she doesn't want to say anything more about it.

"Gretch, I don't want to see you unhappy, and he makes you unhappy."

She smiles at me, trying to make it bright and cheerful, but it falls way short.

"I'm totally happy and completely fine. I promise. I'm just tired. No need to worry about me."

Oh, there's every need to worry. I've seen idiots like him all my life. Controlling, manipulative, mean bullies. I'll never understand why she can't seem to kick him to the curb after knowing him for less than a month.

"Okay, I'll drop it. But I'm here if you need to talk, a place to stay, *anything.* Please promise me if you're ever in trouble, you'll call me right away."

"I promise." It's a whisper. I want to shake her and make her talk to me. But I know that won't work. I have to give her space and let her come to her own conclusions about that loser.

It's a slow Friday morning. The lunch crowd picks up a bit, but it's dead again by the time my new hires arrive, reporting for the afternoon shift. If they were both fully trained, I'd let one of them go home, but for now, I'd like them to work together.

"What are your plans this evening?" Gretchen asks as we leave the café and I head over to my car. Miles is late picking her up.

"Housewarming party for Liam and Ellie up at their

new place," I reply. "It's all decorated the way she wants, and she's ready to show it off. It's just a casual get-together. How about you?"

"I'm not sure what Miles has planned. He said it was a surprise."

"Why don't you sound excited?"

She shrugs, and for the first time, it looks like she might actually admit that there's trouble in paradise. But before she can say anything, a car screeches to a stop in front of us, and the passenger door flings open.

"Get in, babe."

"I hate that guy," I mutter, only for Gretchen to hear.

"I'll see you later," she says and hops into Miles' car. The door shuts, and he tears away, leaving me scowling at the taillights.

When I approach my Honda, I grin, and my mood instantly lifts.

"You didn't have to meet me here."

"Have to? No." Callum's hands are in his pockets as he leans on my vehicle. He has sunglasses on, even though it's overcast. His dark hair is windswept.

I could eat him with a spoon.

"But I missed you today, and I wanted to see you right away."

He pushes off my car and pulls me in for a big hug. Callum's good at hugs. If it were an Olympic sport, which it should be, he'd be a gold medalist.

"How was your day, love?"

"Kind of boring, actually. Now that we're firmly *out* of tourist season, we're slow."

"I can guarantee you that there will be no more boredom for the rest of the day."

I glance around but don't see David. "Where's your detail?"

"Worried for me?"

I just raise a brow, expecting an answer.

"No need to be concerned. He's parked two spaces down and will follow us up to Ellie and Liam's."

"Do you mind driving?" I ask him. "I'm tired, and a little brain dead. I could use the time to gather myself before I'm around a bunch of people."

"Of course, I don't mind." He opens the passenger door for me, and once I'm settled inside, he walks around the car, waves at David, and gets into the driver's seat. "I've never driven a Honda before."

"I'm sure you haven't." I giggle at the thought. "What kind of car *do* you own in London?"

"My favorite is the Porsche. That baby can *move*."

"So, you have more than one?"

"Technically, the royal family owns the entire fleet. I believe there are more than forty vehicles at my disposal."

My tongue sticks to the roof of my mouth. *Forty cars.* Most likely, all luxury vehicles. Because…royalty.

"Well, this won't move like your Porsche, but she does well in the snow and on windy roads."

"Safety is the most important," he says with a wink

and maneuvers us through town and up the mountain road toward Whitetail Mountain Resort, which boasts a world-class ski resort in the winter, and biking and hiking trails in the summer, along with zip lining and other outdoor activities.

Right now, everything is shut down between seasons.

About a mile before the actual resort, Callum turns onto a road that takes us in the opposite direction, toward the other side of the mountain, and then through a gated driveway, staffed by security.

"This feels like a *lot* of security for us," I say with a frown as I take in the number of people milling around the gate. "Did Ellie turn this into a huge party? Because I'm only dressed for the small, informal shindig she told me it was yesterday."

"It's just the family," Callum replies. "I believe Liam invited his friend Sam, and Ellie invited Natasha and Monica. Aside from that, it's just us ."

"Good." I sit back in the seat in relief. I'm in my work clothes, with my hair barely tamed in a long braid down my back and not even a speck of makeup. This was supposed to be a chance to get together with friends, enjoy Ellie's new home, and relax for the evening.

Just what the doctor ordered.

"Maybe Liam's men are training the whole team right now or something, getting ready to take shifts. It just feels like a *lot* of security."

"Hmm," is all he says as he parks in front of the beautiful, brand-new home. When Ellie found it late last year, it was already half-built and owned by the contractor. She took one look at the view of the lake and the house itself and knew she had to have it. And it was early enough that they could customize pretty much everything.

"I hope Natasha made her famous margaritas," I say as David opens my door. "Hi, David."

"Miss," he says with a nod. "I trust you had a pleasant day?"

David's always so formal. I guess that's his job. "It was pleasant enough, thank you. And you?"

He flashes me a smile that reaches his eyes. David likes me. "Quite, thank you."

"How's Alice?"

His eyes warm more at the mention of his wife's name.

"She's well and resting this evening after cooking most of the day for tonight's party."

"Oh, I'm sure we could have had it catered."

"My wife would be absolutely mad if someone suggested such a thing. She's just fine with her feet up now."

"Well, please tell her hello for me."

"It will be my pleasure."

Callum takes my hand, kisses my knuckles, and escorts me to the entrance of the house. I stop short so I can take it all in.

Nestled in tall evergreen trees, the house faces the lake that's a few hundred feet below, and the small mountains on the other side. The neighbors aren't too far away, but I can't see them through the trees.

The house is a craftsman style with a bit of a rustic look to fit in with mountain living. It's big, but not nearly as grand as Sebastian and Nina's place.

"I can't wait to see what they've done on the inside," I say as I start walking again. "The last time Ellie walked me through, it was just drywall and subflooring. She hasn't let me see *anything*."

"She wanted everything to be just so before she unveiled it," Callum replies. "And I can't blame her. It's her first home."

"That's sweet."

We walk through the doors and see that the main level is open concept so we can see through to the floor-to-ceiling windows that show off the incredible view. The living room has vaulted ceilings and is open to the massive black and white kitchen. The fixtures are nickel and industrial. Everything is modern, mixing feminine and masculine elements perfectly, just like Ellie and Liam.

"You're here," Ellie says with a huge smile as she hurries over to give me a hug.

"It looks like we're the last to arrive," I reply, looking around the room. I see Liam, Sam, and Sebastian are out on the balcony talking, Liam pointing at something. Natasha and Monica are mixing margaritas, God bless them.

And Nina is sitting in the living room with—

"Oh, God."

I stumble back a step, sure I must be seeing things. I want to run away. Hide. *Get the hell out of here.*

But before I can do anything at all, Callum pulls me forward.

"Aspen, it's my honor to introduce you to my parents."

Oh, God.

I'm blinking rapidly. Despite having met them briefly at Ellie's wedding, I have no recollection at all of the protocol here, or what I'm supposed to say.

"Aspen," the queen says with a nod.

"Nice to meet you." I hold out my hand to shake and see Nina's eyes go wide.

I'm doing everything wrong.

"Your Majesty." I try again. Ellie hurries behind her parents and quickly shows me how to curtsy. I quickly mimic her, botching it completely, and then simply give up and hang my head in my hands. "I'm so sorry. I just left work, I look awful, and no one warned me. This is what you get from a girl from foster care."

I gasp and look up in horror.

"I can't believe I just said that."

My face is flaming hot, and I wish the floor would open up and swallow me whole. I've made a complete ass out of myself in front of Callum's parents.

And not just any parents. No, these are the freaking king and queen of Britain.

Way to go, Aspen.

"Take a deep breath," the queen says calmly with humor in her eyes as she crosses to me and wraps her arm around my shoulder. I can't even look the king in the eyes. This is *not* how I planned to meet Callum's parents. "Everything is perfectly fine, and you must be beat after a long day of work. There's no need to bother with formalities. This is a casual gathering among family and friends."

"You're very kind," I reply and feel my blood pressure start to lower. "I apologize. Deeply."

"No need." She waves me off, and I finally turn to the king, who's watching me with shrewd, brown eyes like his youngest son's.

"Your Majesty," I say and do a better job with a curtsy this time.

"Ms. Calhoun," he replies. "I do believe you could use a drink."

"Oh, I think you're right about that."

He smiles at me, and I could almost weep with relief. It's no wonder their children are so wonderful; these two are perhaps the best parents I've ever met, no matter their station in life.

They're the kind of mom and dad I always wanted for myself.

Before long, we're swept up in the joy of the party. Ellie gives us all tours of the house. I'm incredibly impressed with the décor, the local artwork she chose, the beautiful paint colors.

"Your designer did an impeccable job," I say when we return to the living area.

"She did. She's here in town. Tate Donovan. If you ever need decorating advice, she's your girl."

"I'll remember that," I reply, knowing that I'll *never* need this kind of decorating help. But I'm thrilled for my friend. "Married life has been good for you."

"It's been wonderful," she agrees and searches the room for her husband. He and Sam have their heads together over by the fireplace, talking intently about something. "Where did Callum and Sebastian go?"

"They're outside, down at the firepit," Natasha says as she and Monica join us. "Ellie, this is the best evening I've had in a long time."

"Same here," Monica adds.

"Not me," I say and hold my hand over my still-queasy stomach. "Why did your parents surprise us all that way?"

"Oh, they didn't," Ellie says. "I think Callum just wanted to surprise *you*."

I feel my eyes narrow. If he were in the room, I'd hunt him down and twist his ear off.

"A surprise for me," I repeat.

"Uh-oh," Monica says. "I've seen that look before. It's the I'm-gonna-kill-someone look."

"Oh, yeah. Someone's gonna die."

But first, I let myself relax and enjoy the food and

the company. The laughter. Despite how the evening started, I do feel relaxed, and I don't even bumble my way through a conversation when the king comes over to talk with me.

"I trust you're enjoying your evening," he says kindly. He's eating some strawberry shortcake.

Seeing him eat dessert makes him more human to me somehow, less...regal.

"I am, thank you. And you?"

"More than I anticipated," he replies. "I didn't know what to expect when we agreed to come for holiday. Of course, I knew that my children had fallen in love with this little piece of the world, and I've seen photographs, but I wasn't sure what the fuss was about."

"And now?"

He sets his empty bowl aside and chews thoughtfully. "It's quite magical here, isn't it?"

"That's a wonderful way to describe it." I smile and sit back, enjoying the king's company. "I felt it the first time I came here, as well. And it was a good thing because I'd loaded up everything I owned and planned to stay."

"Without seeing it first?"

"That's right. I didn't have any family to keep me in Tennessee, and frankly, I needed a fresh start. I'd seen a documentary on Glacier National Park, and I decided to set out and come here to live."

"And it stuck for you."

"Oh, yes. I bought my business not long after I

moved here, and I have wonderful friends. The community has accepted me. For the first time in my life, I can say that I feel like I have roots. That I belong somewhere."

"And isn't that a lovely feeling?" He reaches over to pat my hand.

"Yes, it is. And I have to tell you, I feel that same acceptance from your family, and that's a lovely feeling, as well. Thank you for that."

"You're most welcome. My son has talked about you several times. He's quite taken with you."

"Your son is a special man."

"Indeed."

"Is this where you warn me away?" I ask quietly. His gaze shifts to mine.

"Why would I do that?"

I don't look away from him. "Because he's royalty, and I'm a commoner. I'm as common as it gets, Your Majesty."

"So you think you're not good enough for him?"

I frown. "I didn't say that."

"Didn't you?"

I blow out a breath in frustration. "I worry that you, and the citizens of your country, will think I'm not good enough for him."

"Well, when it comes to the people and their opinions, you'll never win. They can be ruthless in every country, even those I don't rule. Gossip, speculation, rumor, it will all happen, Aspen. And, yes, it can get ugly."

"Callum already warned me of that."

"As he should. Because it's not to be taken lightly, and it takes someone with thick skin to live through it."

"I understand living with a thick skin." I smile, but there's no humor in my voice when I continue. "I've been pointed at, taunted, laughed at for most of my life, and usually not for anything that was my fault or within my control. Well, except getting pregnant at sixteen. That was my fault."

"And how you handled it was also your fault. Which was with dignity, love, and responsibility. You have nothing to be ashamed of, Aspen."

"I'm not ashamed at all." I raise my chin. "So, no, the rumors and speculation don't intimidate me."

"What does intimidate you?"

I glance over at Callum, who's talking with Ellie and Sebastian in the kitchen.

"The three of them have their heads together, most likely cooking up some kind of scheme," I say.

"That's as it's been for most of their lives."

I smile. "I'm intimidated at the thought of losing Callum. Which may sound silly because I don't really *have* him, and I haven't known him long."

"I knew my wife just weeks before we wed. I love her more every day. Time has little to do with it." He waves his hand. "I suspect that you and my son will work things out, Aspen. I'd like to come into your business and enjoy a cup of American coffee sometime."

"I'd love that."

"We'll see that it happens, then." He smiles kindly. Yes, I like Callum's parents very much. "May I give you a piece of advice?"

"Of course."

"When you love someone, losing them is the biggest fear of all. As you well know."

I nod.

"Just live your wonderful life, sweet girl. Every day. Enjoy him and your time together—whether that time spans several months or the rest of your lives. Don't worry so much about the what-ifs, because when you do, it takes away from the joy of today. And time is precious."

"You're right. Thank you for that reminder."

"You're most welcome. Now, go enjoy yourself with people your own age, rather than entertaining an old man."

"I don't see an old man here." I get more comfortable in my chair. "Tell me more about you."

"There are documentaries and books—"

"I'd like to hear it from you," I reply. "I'd like to get to know my new friend."

"Well, then." He clears his throat. "I was actually born in Norfolk…"

CHAPTER 12

~CALLUM~

"I think I might have a bit of a crush on your father," Aspen says once we're safely tucked inside the boathouse for the evening.

"I suspect it's mutual, given the way you two had your heads together for half of the night."

"He's an interesting man," she says and steps out of her trainers. "And I'm not talking about being a king. He enjoys dancing and tending rose bushes. I learned a lot about him this evening that I could never find out in a book or from a documentary."

"I'm glad you enjoyed him." I reach for her, but Aspen steps out of my grasp and props her hands on her hips. "What's this?"

"I may have a soft spot for your father, but *you* are on my shortlist."

I frown. "Whatever for?"

"Callum, you let me walk into an ambush today. I was a complete fool in front of your parents."

"You recovered nicely."

She pinches the bridge of her nose. "That's not the point. The point is, you *knew* they were waiting for us, and you didn't warn me. I was dressed like *this*,"—she points at her T-shirt and jeans—"ready for work, *not* ready to meet the king and queen. Everything I learned about etiquette when I attended Ellie and Liam's wedding flew right out of my head. I was embarrassed and felt inadequate."

"You're not inadequate."

"I was today." She sighs and turns her back on me. "You can't just spring things on me, Callum. Not stuff like that. It's important to me that your family likes me. And I feel like you set me up to fail today."

"That's not what I was doing." I approach her and take her shoulders in my hands. "I would *never* do that to you. I thought it would be a fun surprise to have them here. That's all."

She turns to look up at me, and I see hesitation in her gorgeous green eyes, which makes me feel like a complete arsehole.

"You reminded me that I'm less than."

"No, I invited my parents to come and meet you. Clearly, I went about it all wrong. I should have told you."

"Yeah, you should have. I know this isn't permanent, and who knows, a few months from now, this won't matter, but I deserve to see your *royal* parents with dignity."

"This matters." I move in and cup her cheek. "How can you think that this won't matter? Have I given you the impression that this is a fling for me? That you're some kind of paramour?"

"No." She swallows hard as her pulse hammers in her delicate throat.

I lean in and press my lips there and feel her soften against me. I drag my nose up to her ear and lick her earlobe.

Lifting her easily, I stride into the bedroom and make quick work of our clothes. My hand immediately finds her naked pussy, and I push my fingers inside of her.

"Oh, God," she moans, lifting her hips in invitation.

"This is mine, Aspen." I press my thumb to her clit and watch as she quickly falls into an orgasm. "*Mine.*"

She grabs onto my arm, her short nails digging into my flesh as she writhes beneath me.

How can she think that she doesn't matter? *Everything* I've done over the past month, every decision I've made, has been with her in mind. She is the best part of my life. She's become the single reason I get out of bed each morning.

"You don't just matter," I murmur as I protect us both and then slide inside her, seating myself balls-deep. "You're *everything*, Aspen, and I'll spend every minute of each day reminding you, convincing you, if I have to."

She lifts her legs, wraps them around me, and holds me close as I move faster and faster, chasing the climax I feel gathering in my balls. Jesus, I never stop craving her.

I link my fingers with hers and watch her beautiful face as I fall over the edge into paradise.

When I've caught my breath enough to speak, I press a kiss to her temple. "Tonight won't happen again, love."

"Thank you." She brushes her fingers through my hair. "And, Callum, you're everything for me, too. Which is one of the reasons I was so mortified today. I want to make you proud. I *never* want to embarrass you."

"You don't embarrass me," I assure her. "But I'll also make sure you always have the tools in your arsenal to be comfortable and confident."

"That's all I ask," she says. "Well, that and I could use some sleep."

"I can't promise sleep." I grin and roll us onto our sides, facing each other, still connected. Her eyes widen.

"Already?"

"I'll never get enough of you."

∼

"I NEED YOUR HELP." I'm standing in Monica's beauty salon before they open for the day, watching as she and Natasha place clean towels in a rack above the hair washing bowls.

Monica raises a brow. "You need *our* help?"

"That's right."

"I can't wait to hear this," Natasha says and sits on one of the chairs. "How can we help? If you're about to ask how to dump Aspen gently, I'll remove your genitalia."

I wince. "Not where I'm going with this."

"Good. Proceed."

"Did Aspen mention to you that I bought us a trip to Fiji when we attended the benefit together?"

"She mentioned it," Monica replies.

"Well, I want to take her. In three days."

"You move fast," Natasha says.

"She has new employees that she trusts, and I know Gretchen can handle things for a while," I say.

"You pay attention," Monica says, nodding. "I agree, the café is covered, and if they need any help, I can step in. Natasha and I have both helped out from time to time."

"She's right," Natasha says, "the café won't be an issue, once you talk her into it. She's a bit of a workaholic, so getting her on a plane might be tough."

"Well, I'm planning to propose while we're there, so it needs to happen."

Both women smile at me as if I just proposed to *them.*

"That's so romantic," Monica says.

"Just the sweetest thing ever," Natasha agrees. "You love her. Oh my God, I'm so happy for her."

"I'd like to take her away, have a holiday, and ask her to marry me. We will most likely go to England for a few days before we come back here."

"We've got this," Monica assures me. "You just tell her, don't surprise her because she'll want to make sure everything is squared away at Drips, and we'll do the rest."

"Oh, trust me, I've learned my lesson with surprises. I'll speak with her this evening. Thank you, ladies."

"I can't wait to hear *everything*," Monica says. "We'll plan a girls' night for when you get back."

I laugh and walk out of the salon, with David right behind me, and saunter down the block toward Drips & Sips. I make a quick stop at Brooke's Blooms, buy a bouquet of pink roses, and then walk into the café where I see Aspen glaring at a man from across the counter.

"Why are you here? Gretchen doesn't get off work for another hour."

"I can just hang out here and wait for her. It's a free country."

"It's *my* business, and I can ask you to leave. You won't leave her alone and let her work," Aspen replies. "If you won't go, I'll call the police."

"For what?" he asks, pushing his nose close to Aspen's.

I want to beat the shite out of this wanker, but David shakes his head and steps forward.

"Trespassing," David says as he approaches the man. "She asked you to leave."

"Jesus, this is so fucking stupid. I just want to be with my girlfriend."

"Do you want to go with him?" Aspen asks Gretchen. "However, if you go, you won't be allowed back, Gretch."

"I'm staying," Gretchen says, despite the shit coming out of this arsehole's mouth in response. "I need the job, especially because Miles won't work. Miles, just go home. I'll see you a little later. I'm at *work.*"

"Yeah, so you say," he sneers. "Yesterday, you came home late."

"I went to the grocery store."

"Or you met up with someone for a quick fuck," he says.

"Enough," David says. "Go."

Miles turns and slams out the door.

"I'm so sorry, Aspen," Gretchen says. "I told him to go home, but he just won't listen to me when he gets in these moods."

"He's not welcome back here," Aspen says. "Ever. If he drops you off or picks you up, he waits outside. If he steps foot in here again, I'm calling the police. He's disruptive, rude, and makes a scene every single time, Gretchen."

"I know," Gretchen says. "I'm sorry."

"He can't be worth all of this," I say.

Gretchen's eyes don't meet mine. "He'll calm down and be fine."

"Gretchen," Aspen says, but Gretchen interrupts her.

"I said I was sorry. I have work to do."

She stomps away, and Aspen sighs as she turns to me. "It's been a day already, and I'm only halfway in."

"Anything I can do?"

"Are those for me?"

I remember the roses in my hand and smile as I pass them to her. "Of course, they are."

"Well, these help a lot. Thank you. What are you two up to?"

"Just bringing you flowers," I reply, deciding on the spot to wait to discuss Fiji until after work.

"I have to go home after work today to check my mail and get some clothes and stuff," she says.

"Do you mind if I meet you there?"

"I don't mind at all. I should be home by two."

"I'll see you soon, then."

"Thanks again for the flowers."

"You're welcome."

David and I leave the café. On our way to the car, I say, "We need a background check on that Miles arsehole."

"Already on my list of things to do," he replies.

"Today. I want to know what he ate for breakfast when you're done."

"Yes, sir."

~

David and I pull into Aspen's driveway just behind her. It's a complete coincidence, but a happy one.

"Why is Monica at my house?" Aspen asks when we step out of the car, pointing to what I assume is Monica's Lexus SUV.

"Your guess is as good as mine, love."

David follows us up the steps, and when we walk into the house, it's quiet.

"Where is she?" Aspen wonders, looking around the empty living room and kitchen.

"She does need this."

"Bedroom," I say as Aspen makes a beeline for her boudoir. When we arrive, not only is Monica there, but Natasha, as well. There's a suitcase open on the bed, and clothes piled around it.

"What's going on?" Aspen asks, her hands on her hips.

"Hey!" Natasha says. "We're just packing for you."

"Packing for me for what?"

Monica turns to me. "You didn't tell her?"

"Tell me *what*?"

"Let's go out here and talk, shall we?" I lead Aspen

to the living room. David discreetly leaves through the door to wait in the car.

Smart man.

"Where am I going, Callum?" Aspen asks as she rounds on me. "And let me guess, this is another surprise?"

"I had no idea they were going to take my request of help quite this far," I reply and rub my hand over my face. "I didn't intend for this to be a surprise at all. I bought the vacation to Fiji weeks ago, as you well know."

Her eyes narrow, and I keep talking.

"Now that you're fully staffed at the café, I thought it was a good time for our holiday. Monica assured me that if Gretchen needs anything while you're gone, she or Natasha can step in to help. I just asked them for advice, and they ran with it. I didn't ask them to pack your suitcase."

"She's not going to wear many clothes," we hear Natasha say loudly. "They're just going to have sex the whole time. Why does she need such a big bag?"

"Because, you nitwit, they're going to go out to dinner and stuff. You're the only one who thinks about sex twenty-four-seven."

"No, I'm not. Everyone thinks about sex twenty-four-seven."

"Did you tell them that we're going on vacation to have sex?" Her lips twitch with humor now, and I think the worst of the storm is over.

"I might have implied it." I shove my hands into my pockets. "But, no. Of course, not. But if that's what they want to think, who am I to tell them otherwise?"

"Hmm." She laughs and walks to me to wrap her arms around my waist and press a kiss to my chest. "When is this fabulous holiday happening?"

"In three days."

"Three days." She steps back and shakes her head at me. "Callum, that hardly gives me time to make sure Drips is okay and pack my bags and—"

"No need to worry about your bags." I cup her face and brush my thumb over the apple of her cheek. "Apparently, they have it handled."

"Right."

"I need this with you."

"Why?"

"I don't know. I just do."

"How long will we be gone?"

"Two weeks."

She pales and swallows hard. "I've never left Drips alone for that long."

"I'm not going to say something stupid like *how hard can it be* because I know it's hard, and that it's very important to you. But it's all going to be okay."

"I'm so far outside my comfort zone, I don't even know where it is anymore."

"You can say no."

I can propose in Montana. I don't mind readjusting

my plans in the least if that will make her more comfortable.

Aspen bites her lip as she seems to think it over.

"Oh, and I should mention that we won't be using the commercial airfare that came with the package. We'll be taking a private jet."

Her jaw drops. "I guess I should have realized that."

"What do you say? Are you ready for a holiday?"

"I shouldn't. But yes, I'm ready for some time away with you."

"Excellent." I kiss her lips softly. Just as I lean in to deepen the connection, someone clears her throat.

"Sorry to interrupt. You're all packed, Aspen. You might want to swing by Willa's for a few things, but you're good to go." Monica waves as she and Natasha walk past us and out the front door. "Call me later!"

"You have lovely friends."

"I know." She hugs me again, and I rock her back and forth. "I have the best people in my life. And I'm going to Fiji. I hope they packed my bathing suit."

"I thought you didn't like the water?"

"I can't go to Fiji and *not* snorkel. I think that might be against the law there."

I laugh and kiss the top of her head. "Well, we are law-abiding people."

"Exactly."

CHAPTER 13

~ASPEN~

I have no idea what's happening back home. Drips & Sips could have burned down at this point, and I would have no clue. And right this second, I don't think I care.

It's our last day in paradise. And that's exactly what Fiji is. I'm pretty sure if there's a heaven, I'll see Fiji when I walk through the pearly gates. With the bluest and warmest water ever, warm temperatures, and wonderful people, it might be the best place I've ever been.

We've snorkeled, walked the beach, gone hiking, and had so much sex, my muscles are tired and sore.

I'm not complaining in the least.

Callum is out on a boat, fishing, and I stayed back to spend our last day here in the spa. I've been rubbed and polished, fed, and now I'm soaking in a tub, looking out at the water. I'm loose and relaxed for the first time in maybe my whole life.

Callum brings serenity to my life. Security. He calms me and makes me feel safe. And not because of his wealth or his status but because of who he is. When he says everything will be okay, I believe him because he says it with so much conviction, I know he's right.

This trip was more than a gift. It was magical. I'll never forget it.

And it's not over quite yet.

"Miss Aspen, is there anything else I can do for you today?"

I smile at my personal attendant, Kaneli. She's been wonderful today.

"If you do anything more, I'll never want to leave."

Her smile is bright and full of pride. "I'm happy to hear you enjoyed your day. You're free to soak as long as you want. I've laid your clothes out for you in your room, and you can go whenever you're ready."

"Oh, I have to pay for the services."

"His Highness has already made arrangements. You needn't worry about anything, miss. Enjoy the rest of your day."

She nods and then leaves me alone.

Callum spoils me. It seems to be second nature for him to buy me gifts, to take care of me.

This is all new to me. Greg, even though he was a good husband, didn't pay me this much mind.

Honestly, I didn't realize I was starved for a man's attention until Callum came into my life.

I stand in the tub, let the water drip off me, and then step out and reach for my robe.

Maybe I wasn't starved for attention. Perhaps it was Callum's consideration that I needed. Because frankly, the idea of another man coming into my life doesn't interest me in the least.

I walk into the private room assigned to me when I arrived—no shared locker room in this joint—to find my clothes are indeed waiting for me. Upon further inspection, it looks like they've been washed and pressed.

Even my underwear, which I wore on this trip because…you just never know.

I've never stayed somewhere fancy enough for them to wash my clothes for me. I wonder if this is the resort that was offered in the auction, or if Callum upgraded us.

I dress and walk along the windy path above the water to get to our suite, followed discreetly by security. Our room is a hut suspended over the ocean. We can see fish below us, and we have a rope hammock thing to sit on, also over the water.

I think I could live here.

Of course, then I'd take it all for granted, and it would become old hat. I wouldn't appreciate it nearly as much as I do right now.

No, I'll just have to work my ass off and save my money so I can visit often.

I key in the code to our suite and let myself in. The security guard assigned to me will stand guard outside.

I step out of my flip-flops and turn, then stop cold. Pink rose petals are sprinkled on the floor, leading through to our bedroom. I eagerly follow them and feel tears fill my eyes when I take in the scene before me.

Pink roses are everywhere. The bed is littered with petals, and more are on the floor here, leading out to the balcony.

Callum's sitting in a lounge chair, clad only in swimming trunks. His torso is bare and tanned, his muscles toned under smooth skin. His arms are up under his head, and his feet are crossed on the lounge chair.

"Well, don't you look relaxed?"

I don't sit next to him. I climb onto his lap and rest my head on his shoulder. Touching him without hesitation, as if he's *mine*, is something I've grown used to—and enjoy.

"Thanks for this week," I murmur.

"I can say, without a doubt, it's been the best week of my life." He kisses my head and drags his fingertips up and down my arm. "We'll have to do it often."

"I was just thinking while I was at the spa that I could come here regularly. I'll have to make a Fiji fund jar and squirrel away my tips."

"Hmm," is all he says in response. I can tell, just from that little reply, that it irritated him.

"I don't expect you to take me on vacation all the time." I kiss his jawline.

"I'll take you on holiday, Aspen. I quite enjoy it."

"I'm not with you because of the money, or the trips, or the roses. Although, the roses are nice."

"If I thought that was the case, we wouldn't be here. In fact, I think you're with me *despite* all of that."

"Maybe."

He kisses my hair again and then shifts so he's facing me. "I know that the press has always painted me as the playboy prince. As irresponsible, spontaneous, and carefree. I let them believe that about me because it was easier to just flash a smile than try to defend myself, especially when the rumors weren't true. I knew the truth, and my family knew, and that's all that mattered."

I frown and lace my fingers with his, wondering where this is going.

"I'm a planner, Aspen. An overthinker. I usually make a schedule for things and stick to it. And I had a plan for this. But being here with you like this right now, open and raw, sharing our feelings, is the appropriate time to lay it all on the line.

"I knew the minute I saw you standing in my brother's kitchen two years ago that you were going to change my life. I felt a connection to you that I simply couldn't explain. And then I messed everything up, and it took me *years* to fix it."

"Callum—"

"Let me finish, love. You are everything wonderful in my life, and I love you so completely, so madly that it's an ache in my chest. Your passion for life, your work ethic, your humor, they all breathe life into *me.* Being with you has made me a better person, and I never want to lose you. So, I'm asking you here, in this beautiful place—

"Wait." He scurries off the chair and kneels next to me, holding my hand.

Holy shit.

Prince Callum Wakefield is going to ask me to *marry him.*

"I'm asking you here, in this beautiful place, if you'll do me the honor of becoming my wife. Spend your life with me, Aspen. I promise you I'll remind you every single day how much I love you and how grateful I am to have you in my life."

I lick my lips as Callum pulls a ring out of his pocket and offers it to me.

"Callum." His name is a whisper on my lips. I can only imagine the complications that will come with marrying royalty. Will I have to sell my café? Will I have to move to London? How will everything happen?

But as I stare into his brown eyes, so hopeful and full of love, I know that I'd do all of those things and more to be with him for the rest of my life.

"I have so many questions," I admit as I lean in to rest my forehead on his. "And before I answer, I need to tell you that I love you, too. We haven't said the *L*-word before now."

"I love you so much, Aspen."

"Yes, I will marry you, Callum."

He leans back and stares at me as if he's surprised.

"Did you think you'd have to talk me into it?"

"Honestly, yes." He laughs and slides the ring, this stunning emerald ring with diamonds, on my finger, then pulls me in for a soft, romantic kiss.

"Holy shit, we're getting married," I say against his lips.

He urges me to my feet and tugs me into the bedroom.

"These flowers were a nice touch, by the way."

"That was the resort because they know it's our last night here," he replies and kisses my shoulder as he pushes my sundress off and lets it pool around my feet.

Aside from my panties, I'm standing naked in front of him.

"I wasn't planning to get married again," I admit to him. I'm naked, and this is the time for confessions. "Not to anyone. Because loving someone that much means setting yourself up for loss."

"Sweetheart, I can't even imagine the pain you've been through. The thought of losing you that way isn't fathomable."

"I wanted to die, too." He pulls me in to hug me close,

skin to skin. "And then you happened. I wasn't ready for you years ago, Callum. Even if we'd started dating then, it wouldn't have worked because I hadn't finished healing yet. And I certainly would have run in the other direction if you'd proposed. I needed time. And maybe hanging on to the anger is what gave me that time."

"And now?"

"Now, I can't imagine my life without you in it. I know everything is about to change big time. That it's not as simple as you moving to Montana and us living a quiet life in my little house with my little business."

"I wish it was that simple. For your sake."

"I'm marrying all of you. The man and the prince. And you have important responsibilities that I admire very much. We'll figure it out."

"You're a wonderful woman, Aspen. I'm a lucky bloke."

I grin as his mouth descends to mine, and with all of the words we needed to speak spoken for now, we fall onto the bed. Instead of the frenzied, intense sex I've come to expect from him, Callum's hands are gentle, almost lazy as he glides his fingers up my side to my breast.

His lips wrap around the nipple as his hand travels down my belly to my core.

If intense sex with this man is fabulous, gentle sex is out of this fucking world.

"If you're trying to kill me, it's working."

"I'm enjoying you," he whispers and kisses my chin. "Your skin, your scent. The raspy tone of your voice when you're turned on."

"I'm damn turned on."

"I know." He's at my side, not nestled between my legs. And rather than shift, he lifts my leg and guides himself into me. "So slick, so perfect."

"Holy shit." This position is new, and the angle is *ridiculous.* I reach down to press on my clit as he moves in a slow rhythm, set to drive us both mad.

I've never felt so exposed, so *linked* to another human being as I do at this moment.

Callum kisses my shoulder, and I feel the tension begin to build, low in my belly.

"I'm going over."

"Yes, darling." He moves just a bit harder, a smidge faster, and that's all it takes to push me into the orgasm. I bear down, and he follows me over, then pulls me into his arms, holding me tightly.

I glance down at my left hand.

I've only ever worn a simple gold band on that finger. And now, it's a huge emerald.

"That was Queen Victoria's," he says casually and brings it up to his lips for a kiss.

"I can't wear this."

"Why ever not?"

"Callum, it's priceless. What if the stone gets lost or stolen?"

"Given that it will stay on your hand, and you have constant security, I'd say it being stolen is unlikely."

"This is a family heirloom."

"Indeed. And it's staying in the family. My father gave it to me to give to you. He brought it with him to Montana."

I stare at him, stunned. "What?"

"That's why they made the trip. I originally asked them to send a royal courier with a ring for you, but Mum and Father decided to come themselves. I told him I wanted an emerald because they remind me of your eyes, and he chose this from the family vault."

"Callum."

"If you don't like it, I'm sure we can choose something else. Or have something made."

"Of course, I like it. My God, look at it. This stone must be ten karats."

"Twenty-one, actually."

My first instinct is to take it off and give it back. Not the proposal, but the ring.

"The girl from the wrong side of the tracks is wearing Queen Victoria's ring."

"Don't ever refer to yourself that way again, Aspen. You're not less than because of where you come from."

"You're right. But this is *insane.*"

"There's a matching tiara that will be on loan to you from the Crown whenever we appear in an official capacity. After we're married, of course."

"Of course." I shake my head. "I'm already overwhelmed."

"I know." He kisses my temple. "I'd like to go to London when we leave here tomorrow so you can see Frederick and his wife. You'll also meet Mary, who was the lady in waiting for my sister most of her life. She also helped Nina extensively when she became engaged to Sebastian."

"That'll help. Can we think about all of that tomorrow? For today, I just want to enjoy our last day of vacation like a normal couple who just got engaged."

"I think that's a marvelous idea." He shifts over me and kisses me down the middle of my chest. "I do believe a *normal* couple would make love again. Don't you?"

"Probably. At least once more. Maybe twice."

"Your wish is my command, sweetheart."

CHAPTER 14

~CALLUM~

We've been on the plane for twenty bloody hours. Aspen and I are both knackered when we arrive in London and endure a short drive to the palace where my flat is.

I'm excited to have her here for a few days to show her where I live and what I love about London. She's been to the palace before, when Ellie and Liam wed last year, but this is a whole new experience for both of us.

"That was the longest flight of my life," she says as she leans her head on my shoulder.

"We'll get home and take a nap." I kiss her hair, breathing in her scent.

"I'm exhausted," she says, yawning. "But I want to see everything."

"You've been here before."

"I was in and out for the wedding. I arrived the afternoon before and had to leave the morning after. I had just hired Gretchen and didn't want to leave Drips for long, but I wouldn't have missed the wedding for the world."

"So you didn't do any sightseeing when you were here?"

"No, but I did get to see parts of the palace that others don't, and that was cool."

"Well, you'll certainly do that again, but I'd like to show you other things, as well. Some of my favorite things."

"I love the sound of that. Are your parents here?"

"No, they're still in Montana."

She looks up at me in surprise. "Really?"

"Yes. It seems they've fallen in love with it there and wanted to look around for a while. They'll probably be there when we get back."

"Oh, that would be wonderful. I'd love to see them again."

We drive past the crowds and through the gate, then around to the back of the palace where we're out of sight from prying eyes. This is the entrance the family uses most often when coming and going.

David escorts us to my flat, and once we're behind closed doors, Aspen wraps her arms around me for a hug.

Being held is important to her, and something I'm happy to indulge.

"David's been away from Alice for quite a while," she says.

"We'll be back in less than a week. Travel is a part of his job, and they knew that when they got married."

"I know." She leans back and smiles up at me. "It was only an observation."

"Before we get married, we'll assign a personal detail to you, as well. In the meantime, you'll stick close to me."

"I'm certainly not planning to drift far from you, especially while we're here." She kisses my chin just as a knock sounds on the door. "I thought we had time to rest?"

"I need to introduce you to someone first. It won't take long."

I open the door and am immediately hugged, my cheek pinched.

Only Mary could get away with this.

"Callum, my sweet boy," she says. "You've been gone too long."

"Well, I'm home now, and I brought someone for you to meet."

Mary, at sixty-something years old, retired, and grandmotherly, turns to Aspen.

"Why, miss, you're dead on your feet."

"Sweetheart, this is Mary. If there's something you wish to know about protocol, being a royal, etiquette, or anything else you may need, Mary knows. She's been with us for most of her life. Certainly, all of mine."

"I was there when this one was born," she confirms.

Mary's been a second mother to my siblings and me. We adore her.

"Well, then, I'm sure I have a million questions for you," Aspen says.

"Mary, it's my pleasure to introduce you to my fiancée, Aspen Calhoun."

"You're just lovely," Mary says and then takes Aspen's shoulders in her hands. "I just know we're going to be fast friends. I'm here to help, to teach you, and to assist with anything you might need. But first, I'm going to start a nice hot shower for you, and then we'll get you nice and comfortable for a long nap. You've had a long journey."

Aspen glances back at me with surprised eyes. "Where will you be?"

"I'll be here," I assure her. "I'll see you in a few minutes."

Mary whisks her away to fuss over her, the way she fussed over the rest of us all of our lives, and I wander through my flat. The kitchen is freshly stocked with my favorite things. I have two bedrooms and three bathrooms in my six-thousand-square-foot place, along with a lap pool, a media room, and an office.

It's too much space for me, but it's the smallest flat in the palace.

I wander into the guest bathroom since Mary and Aspen are currently using the master, and take a hot shower of my own, changing into sweats and a T-shirt after. When I walk back into the living room, I find my gorgeous fiancée sitting on the sofa.

"Where's Mary?" I ask.

"She said she'd be back later after we've had time to rest. I didn't realize it's barely noon."

"Jet lag is a bugger." I pull her to her feet, but when she simply shuffles after me, I lift her into my arms and carry her into my bedroom. "Do you know how many times I've daydreamed about having you in my bed?"

"No."

I smile and kiss her pouty lips. "I lost count. When you were in this house last year for the wedding, I had to stop myself from abducting you from your room and hauling you back here, caveman-style."

"I wouldn't have enjoyed it nearly as much then as I would now."

I tuck her under the covers and climb in beside her. "And now you're here with me."

"Hmm." She turns around so she can bury her face in my chest whilst she sleeps. "And when I wake up, I'm going to seduce you in your bed."

"I'll hold you to that, love."

∾

"Callum."

I can tell by the sound of her voice that I'm in trouble. I just have no idea what on earth for.

"Yes?"

"Can you come in here, please?"

I join Aspen in the walk-in closet that is exclusively hers and raise a brow. "Yes?"

"Why do I have a closet full of clothes here? A closet the size of my first apartment, I might add."

"I didn't know you lived in a studio apartment."

"This is more the size of a two-bedroom, and you're changing the subject. Why do I have all of this?"

"Because when I called ahead and told the staff we were coming, they set this all into motion."

"*Why*? What's wrong with my clothes?"

"Nothing, but you don't have enough of them. The same was done for Nina when she came to the palace."

"I don't understand."

I pull my mobile out of my pocket and FaceTime my sister-in-law.

"This is a nice surprise," Nina says when she answers. "Are you having a wonderful trip?"

"We are, thank you for asking. But Aspen is concerned about the clothes that have been made for her—"

"*Made for me?*"

"—and I was hoping you could have a word with her."

"Of course. Put her on."

I pass the cell to Aspen, who immediately starts asking questions.

"Nina, what in the hell? I don't need all of this.

We're only here for a few days. And how did they know my size?"

"Okay, friend, take a deep breath," Nina interrupts. "First of all, you *do* need them, and more. Congratulations, by the way."

"Thanks."

"You'll attend events that you need to be dressed appropriately for. I know you're drop-dead gorgeous in your jeans and T-shirts, but that won't fly when you're appearing in an official capacity. You need suits. Also, pants aren't really acceptable."

Aspen's eyes narrow on mine. "What do you mean?"

"I mean that when you're in public, you have to wear skirts or dresses."

"Like hell."

"Hey, I don't make the rules. Privately, you can wear whatever you want."

"Gee, thanks."

I shrug and smile as Aspen continues peppering Nina with questions.

"Why didn't anyone warn me?"

"Think about it, Aspen," Nina says. "Have you ever seen Ellie or me in jeans when we're being photographed?"

"No, I guess not."

"Trust me, the clothes are the best you can buy. They're gorgeous and will fit you like a glove. And don't even get me started on the shoes. I'm getting all hot and bothered."

Aspen laughs, and I feel my stomach loosen.

"Okay. I guess. Mary's going to work with me over the next few days."

"You'll love her. Please tell her hello for me. And, Aspen, just relax and soak it in. No one will quiz you, and we'll all help you as time goes on. I'm still learning, too. Oh, and just let that whole article roll off your back. It's ridiculous, and people say stupid things."

Aspen's eyes fly to mine, and I hurry away to fetch my iPad. What in the bloody hell is she talking about?

"I haven't seen an article," I hear Aspen reply.

"Oh. Well, when you do, put on your thick skin and remember that they don't know you, and they never will. Keep your chin up. I'm going to hug you properly when you get home. I'm so excited for you, my friend."

"Thank you. I'll probably call again for more advice."

"I'm here anytime," Nina assures her before hanging up, and Aspen passes my mobile back to me.

"What article?" Aspen asks.

The image on the screen, along with the headline, have me raging on the inside. I want to tear someone apart.

But I remain calm and turn it for her to see.

"Prince Callum to wed poor American widow: a rags to riches story." She raises a brow and looks at me. "Well, they work fast."

"Bloody vultures," I mutter and take the tablet away,

turn it off, and toss it onto the bed. "She's right, ignore them."

"I have more important things to think about," she says, waving it off. "I've been here less than twenty-four hours, and it's already painfully obvious that I'm way underqualified for this."

"We all are. But you'll learn. The most important part, the loving-me part, you have down to a science."

"You say pretty things just to appease me."

"Did it work?"

"Sort of." She rubs her hand over her face. "What do we have for today?"

"Lunch with Freddy and Catherine. That's it. And tomorrow, we have the ribbon cutting for the hospital in Edinburgh."

"Lunch with the heir to the throne and ribbon cuttings." She laughs and sits on the bench in the middle of the closet. "Custom-made designer clothes. And a prince."

"It's a lot."

"It's massive," she agrees. "And you're right. I'll learn. But damn, Callum, I had no idea. Am I going to have to give up Drips & Sips?"

"No." I sit next to her and take her hand. "Owning a business isn't against any rule. You may have to hire a general manager to oversee it for you because there will be some travel for us, but it's my goal to live in Montana as much as possible."

"What about your responsibilities here?"

"We'll figure it out. I can work remotely for a lot of it."

"Will I need to sell my house?"

"Do you want to?"

She bites her lip. "I don't think I do. I love that house. I know it's not fancy, but it's mine."

"Then we won't sell. You have plenty of space and buildings for security. I like your home."

"You don't want something fancier?"

"Aspen, I want *you*. And I want you to be happy. If living in your lovely Montana home makes you happy, that's where we'll live. Yes, there's a lot of pomp and circumstance that comes with marrying a member of the royal family, but let's not lose sight of the heart of this, shall we? It's you and me. We're two people who love each other. We make the rest fit into that."

"I like that. And I needed the reminder. Thank you."

"Now, choose something to wear, and we'll go see my brother."

"How formal is lunch?"

"Not formal. I'll be wearing slacks and a button-down shirt."

"So, a casual dress is appropriate?"

"Yes."

"Okay, I'll be ready in thirty minutes."

"You're lovely." I kiss Aspen's hand as we walk down the hall to the dining room to meet Freddy and Catherine. "Green is your color."

"Of course, it is, I'm a redhead." She smiles up at me and then looks a bit nervous as we reach the dining room's threshold.

"You've already met him," I remind her.

"That was different." She takes a deep breath. "But let's do this."

Frederick and Catherine are already waiting for us and stand to greet us warmly.

"Your Highness," Aspen says to Freddy, who smiles warmly and takes her hands in his.

"Aspen, it's lovely to see you again. We're about to be family, so please, call me Freddy."

"Thank you."

"And you remember my wife, Catherine."

"Of course."

"How is Montana?" Catherine asks. "Your parents are staying for a while, so they must be enjoying it."

"It sounds that way," I agree. "It's beautiful there."

"You should come and visit," Aspen says. "I think you'd enjoy it. And your children would love all of the outdoor activities."

"It's certainly on our list of places for a holiday," Freddy says.

"Well, if nothing else, you'll get to see it when we get married." Aspen grins, and my brother's startled eyes find mine.

We haven't started to plan the wedding yet, but obviously, Aspen assumes we'll marry in Montana.

"I honestly don't know if that's possible," I say, sitting back in my chair thoughtfully.

"If what's possible?" Aspen asks.

"Marrying out of the country. I don't think a royal descendant ever has. Do you, Freddy?"

"Not that I'm aware of," he says. "But that doesn't mean it's out of the question."

"I hadn't considered having a huge wedding like Liam and Ellie," Aspen says. "It's just not my style."

"I understand," Catherine says. "Were you thinking a smaller, country wedding?"

"Yes, with close family and friends, and no press."

"Well, this might take some convincing for Father," Freddy says. "The citizens will be disappointed if they don't get well-publicized nuptials."

"What if it's a compromise?" Catherine asks. "A small, private ceremony and a party in Montana, and then a larger reception later here in London?"

"It sounds like the perfect scenario," I agree and reach for Aspen's hand. "What do you think?"

"It's definitely a good compromise. I'm sorry I assumed. I guess I'm still getting used to everything. I've never had to worry about the press before."

"We have people to worry about the press for us," Freddy says with a wink. "You just live your life, Aspen."

"That's my plan."

∼

It's been a busy week for her. I can see the exhaustion in her eyes as we take the helicopter to Edinburgh for the hospital opening. She's absolutely beautiful in a navy-blue dress, her hair loose around her shoulders.

This is our first official public event together. I know she's nervous, but there's no need to be.

"Just smile and wave," I remind her. "They're not allowed to touch you or ask for a photo with you. You can shake hands if you like."

"Got it." She nods and offers me a reassuring smile. I've already run through the schedule of events, and we should be in and out in just over an hour. We'll get a tour of the facilities and meet with some of the patients. Then I'll cut the ribbon, we'll pose for photos, and call it a day.

"Are you ready to go back to Montana?"

"Will it hurt your feelings if I say yes?"

"Not in the least. I'm ready to get back myself."

The helicopter touches down on the helipad of the roof of the hospital, and we're escorted inside. The next hour is filled with a tour, meeting patients, and posing for photos.

Aspen is wonderful with the patients, asking questions, and engaging with them. She has a knack for speaking with strangers, which is probably one of the reasons Drips & Sips does so well.

Finally, we're escorted outside to the front of the

building where the paparazzi are camped out, waiting to take photos of me cutting the ribbon and making a speech.

Having Aspen by my side for all of it is the best feeling ever.

Just as we turn to leave, one of the media members, someone I've known for a long time, calls out to us.

"I never pegged you as someone gullible enough to fall for a gold digger, Callum."

I turn back and narrow my eyes at the man, who's currently smirking at me. The crowd has gone silent, waiting for my response.

"Mr. Parsons is now permanently removed from the media ticket," I announce to my team. "And if anyone else has anything inflammatory to say about my fiancée, speak up now so I know who to blackball."

No one else says a word as we turn to walk away. I hear Parsons complaining behind me, but I don't turn to engage with him further.

Because if I did, I'd likely break his blasted nose.

"Let it roll off, remember?" Aspen whispers to me and squeezes my hand. "They don't matter."

"I want to kick his arse," I mutter. "And yes, I realize I need to follow my advice. I'll get there."

"Let's go home, Callum."

"That's the best idea I've heard all day."

CHAPTER 15

~ASPEN~

I've been back in Montana for seventy-two hours, and I'm slammed. Gretchen hasn't been in to work since I arrived, calling out every single day. Wendy and Rachel are both on vacation, a scheduling snafu made by me, so it's just Paula and me here.

"Paula, I need you to go see if we have more scones in the back."

My new hire, who's been here for a month and should be fully trained by now, blinks at me. "Are those still on the second shelf?"

I take a deep breath so I don't snap at her. I don't *want* to snap at her. We all learn at different paces, and she's excellent with the customers. But this is *not* the week for this.

"Yes, ma'am. Just grab everything that's there. I don't know why we're so busy today, but everyone in town has decided this is the hot spot, and we're shorthanded."

"Okay." She hurries into the stock room, and I turn to the next customer in line, surprised to see my fiancé standing before me.

"Well, hello."

His eyes narrow on me. "What's wrong?"

"I'm just busy, and Gretchen called out. Again. My other two employees are on vacation, and Paula's great, but she's not speedy." I take a breath and offer Callum a smile. "But it's really nice to see you. How are you?"

"On duty." He nods to David, and both men roll up their sleeves.

"No, you don't have to help."

Callum marches behind the counter and tips my chin up with his finger. "We're a team now, darling. I won't leave here knowing that you're drowning in work, any more than you'd let me stand in front of fire-breathing media by myself."

"Are you still mad at that man?"

"Hell, yes."

I take his hand and kiss his palm. "I love you."

His eyes soften, and he leans in to kiss my forehead. I have a line of people, and no time for this, but it feels so damn good.

"What can I do for you, love?"

"I'm here, too," David says. "I'm going to clear and clean some empty tables if that suits you, ma'am."

"That's incredible, David, thank you."

"And me?" Callum asks.

"Can you check on Paula to see what in the hell is taking her so long to grab more scones?"

"On it. Take another deep breath, darling."

He scurries away, and I turn to find Mrs. Blakely, the owner of Little Deli just down the street, smiling at me.

"He's a handsome one," she says with a wink.

"It's sort of absurd how handsome he is," I say with a sigh. "Sorry to keep you waiting. Things are a little nuts in here today."

"Oh, I'm just fine. Watching you two lovebirds together is a balm to my cynical soul. That's a beautiful ring, Aspen. Congratulations."

"Thank you." I glance down at the green stone shimmering in the light of my café. Every time I look down at it, I'm always surprised that any of this is real. "What can I do for you, Mrs. Blakely?"

"Well, I've been craving a white mocha, and I'd love a huckleberry scone if you have any left."

"I sent Paula back to check. Let me go see what's keeping her. I'll be right back."

I rush to the back room and find Callum glaring at Paula, whose head is down, her hands linked behind her back.

"What's going on?"

"She was stealing," he says. "I caught her red-handed with her hands in the safe."

"It was just until payday," Paula says. "Tips aren't

covering my bills, and I just needed something to hold me over until Friday."

"Get out," I say immediately. "I don't have time to deal with this shit, Paula. You're done. If you'd just come to me and asked me for an advance, I would have happily done so. Instead, you're fired. Get your things and go."

"But we're so busy."

"I've handled far worse, Paula. This is my business. And Callum's here to help. He's not going to steal from me."

She grabs her purse and jacket and quietly leaves.

"I'm sorry, Aspen," Callum says.

"It's not the first time, and it won't be the last. I have customers." I grab the scones off the shelf and hurry back to my job. Callum jumps right in, fetching food out of the glass case while I fill coffee orders. David keeps the dining room clean as customers leave so new ones can fill the seats.

We have it down to a science by the time we're done for the day.

"Let me take you home, and I'll rub your feet," Callum says. He's massaging my shoulders while I clean the espresso machine.

"That sounds wonderful, but I can't. I have to go to my house. Natasha, Monica, Ellie, and Nina are coming over for girls' night. They want to hear about our trip and the proposal. Monica and Natasha haven't even seen my ring yet."

"Raincheck on the foot rub, then." Callum kisses my neck, just below my ear.

"For sure. I have interviews set up over the next few days for potential general managers. I figure, the sooner I get someone in here, the better—if for no other reason than to help me out. We're never this busy during the off-season."

"You've made this place something special, Aspen. The locals enjoy it as much as the tourists."

"And that makes me happy. So, I'll be pretty busy over the next few weeks. I hope we don't have anywhere we need to be."

His lips turn up into a smile. "Nothing that can't be rescheduled."

"Thank you."

"We're both making adjustments and compromises, love. We'll get everything figured out. It's just going to take a little time."

~

"You know," Ellie says later that night, "it says something that Father chose the Queen Victoria emerald for you."

I take my first sip of Natasha's margarita and then set it aside.

"Is something wrong with it?" Natasha asks.

"No, why?"

"You scrunched up your nose."

"My stomach's been off for the past couple of days. I think it's just jet lag and stress. Mostly stress. I think I'll sip on some water for a bit."

"Have some food, too," Monica suggests.

"Sorry, Ellie, keep going," I say, turning back to my friend.

"Well, that particular set is my father's favorite of the family jewels. He's loaned it out before, mostly to my mother for important dinners and such. He actually brought a selection of rings with him to Montana and made the final decision on what Callum should propose with after he met you."

"I love your father," I admit to her. "We got along so well, and I loved hearing about his childhood and some of the shenanigans he got up to as a teenager. How he met your mother. We talked for a long time."

"I know. I saw," Ellie says. "And he might have a little crush on you, I think. After you both left on your holiday, he spoke of you a few times. And the fact that you have that emerald on your finger tells me that he not only approves of Callum marrying you, but he also trusts and respects you."

I feel tears fill my eyes. It's been a hell of a few days, and hearing this makes me feel good.

"The feeling is mutual."

"How did Callum propose?" Nina asks. "Also, holy shit, Natasha, these margaritas are ridiculously delicious."

"I know," Natasha says with a smug grin.

"He proposed in Fiji," I say. "On the balcony of our hut. It was kind of spontaneous and sweet. And sexy."

"I know that smile," Monica says, pointing at me. "You're totally boning a prince."

"Oh, yeah," I reply with a nod. "A lot, actually."

"This is not a lovely conversation." Ellie's face is scrunched in a scowl. "Let's skip the sex parts."

"No, tell us *everything* about the sex parts, for those of us not having any sex," Natasha says.

"You're the only one in this room not getting any," Monica reminds her. "Sorry, babe."

"It sucks."

"Let's just say, he can't keep his hands off me, and the feeling is entirely mutual. Then we went to London, where I was given more clothes than any one person should have, and took some etiquette lessons from Mary."

"Mary's the best," Ellie says. "And she knows *everything*."

"She's maybe the kindest woman in the world," Nina adds.

"I agree. She was wonderful, and I had a lot of questions. And I kept messing things up. I don't want to embarrass Callum."

"Sebastian gave me some good advice when we first got together," Nina says. "He and his siblings are taught to be members of the royal family from the day they're born. It's ingrained in them. For you and I, we're starting from scratch, taking a crash course. It's not easy, but I can assure you, it's worth it. And things will come easier and faster as time goes on."

"Are you moving to London?" Monica asks.

"We're going to split our time between there and here, hopefully spending more time in Montana than not. We're keeping this house, and security will set up in the barn, most likely. It'll have to be converted into a second house, of course. So, hopefully, we can get the permits for that from the city."

"There's a lot to think about," Natasha says. "What about Drips?"

"I'll hire a manager to take over for me. That one stings a bit, I admit. I'm proud of my business, and I enjoy being there every day. But we're both making compromises. Hopefully, I'll still be able to maintain an active role in the café."

"Everything will smooth out with some time," Nina assures me. "It helps that he's not the heir."

"She's right," Ellie adds. "He has duties and jobs of his own, but you'll make it work."

"Hey, couples make it happen all the time," Monica says. "The only difference here is that he's a prince."

"A hot prince," I add with a laugh. "It feels good to be able to talk to you guys about this. I panicked a bit while we were gone, wondering what in the hell I thought I was doing. But every time I look at him, I go all gooey inside. I know I could survive without him, but I don't want to go through life without him. We're connected, you know?"

Three heads nod yes, and Natasha frowns.

"I hope I get it one day," she says. "But in the meantime, I'm so happy for you, friend. And proud of you. You're a badass."

"Damn right, I am."

Just as we're laughing, I hear a knock.

"Maybe Callum couldn't wait to see you," Nina suggests as I walk to the door.

But when I open it, it's not Callum.

"I need your help." The words are whispered through swollen, bloody lips.

"Oh my God, Gretchen." I lead her gently inside as the others gather around us.

"I'm sorry to interrupt. I just didn't know where else to go."

"Don't be silly," Monica says. "What happened to you, sweetheart?"

"Miles." My voice is hard as stone. Gretchen nods. "You're done with him, here and now, Gretch."

"I want to be. I just don't know how to leave him. He threatens me all the time. Aspen, I'm not this girl. He's been controlling and mean since the week he moved into my apartment. He said if I leave him, he'll kill my parents."

"Motherfucker," Natasha growls. "Let's cut off his fucking balls."

Gretchen's crying softly now. Her left eye is swollen shut. Her nose is puffy and split on one side. She winces as she sits on the couch.

"Ribs?" I ask.

"I think he broke a couple. He got mad at me because I told him I was going to work tomorrow. He wants me to stay home with him, but we don't have any money. Every penny I make, he spends. I'm about to be evicted from my apartment, and he doesn't care. He doesn't love me at all."

"No, honey," Nina says as she walks in with a wet rag to dab at Gretchen's wounds. "He doesn't love you. Anyone who can do this to you doesn't love you at all."

"How did you get away?" Ellie asks.

"He fell asleep, and I just left. I walked here because I couldn't risk starting the car and waking him. If he finds me, he'll kill me. I know it."

"Why is your voice so raspy?" I ask, already knowing the answer to that question.

"He choked me out."

"Jesus," Monica whispers. "He needs to be in jail. Aspen—"

"Absolutely," I agree.

"No," Gretchen says, shaking her head. "It'll only make things worse."

"No, it won't," Natasha insists. "Gretchen, you have to press charges and put this asshole in jail. He'll keep doing this to you—or to someone else."

"He tried to kill you," I say. "It's not just domestic abuse, it's attempted murder."

A tear falls down Gretchen's cheek.

"I just wanted to find someone to love me."

"And you will, sweet girl." I wrap my arm around her shoulders and gently hug her. "You will. This isn't love. This is evil. We're going to do something about it."

"I'm calling Liam," Ellie says. "He'll know what to do."

"We have three security guards sitting outside," Monica reminds us all.

"Don't you worry," I assure Gretchen. "There's no way that bastard's getting near you now. You'll stay here for a while, and we'll put a man on the house, keeping you safe."

"You'd do that?"

"Of course, we'd do that," Ellie says. "I'm calling Liam."

∽

"Gretchen's in bed," I say to Callum several hours later. We called an ambulance for her and met the police at the hospital where Gretchen was questioned, evaluated, and taken care of before she was released to us. I sit next to him with a sigh. "I'm exhausted."

"Did the police arrest that fucker?"

His voice is hard, but his lips gentle when he kisses my head.

"Yeah. They said he'll likely be out on bail tomorrow, so keeping security here for a couple of days until she can leave the state is important. I think he'll try to come after her."

"Agreed," Callum says. "We'll keep someone with her for as long as she needs."

"Thank you. I'm going to send her to her sister's place in Portland next week. She'll be safe there and can start to heal. I feel awful for her, Callum. I feel so guilty."

"Why on earth do you feel guilty?"

"Because I saw from the beginning what a creep he was. I *knew* he was bad news, and I didn't do anything beyond telling her he was a douche. I should have done something more."

"There was nothing more to do. She's a grown woman who made a choice to continue seeing him. And then she got trapped in a horrible situation. I'm just relieved that she has you and trusts you enough to come here and ask for help."

"Me, too."

"Come on, sweetheart. Let's get you to bed. We've done all we can do for tonight."

"If we stay here, David has to stay, too."

"I love that you think of the staff and their needs, but this is what he's paid to do, darling. David's fine. I'll let him know we're staying."

I kiss his cheek. "I'm grateful that I found you and that you're so wonderful."

He pulls me close and rocks me back and forth. "I feel the same way, my love."

CHAPTER 16

~CALLUM~

Getting up early isn't new to me. I've always been a morning person, so rising before the sun to help Aspen at her café isn't an inconvenience. I just hate that she had to get up so early after being up late worrying after Gretchen.

We dropped Aspen off at Drips & Sips, and then David brought me back to the boathouse so we could shower and change before joining Aspen once more to work through the day.

If you asked me a few months ago if I ever thought I'd be serving coffee in a small town in Montana, I would have laughed.

And now, it seems there's nowhere else I'd rather be.

Catching Paula with her hands in the safe yesterday filled me with rage. But Aspen handled it the way she handles everything, with professionalism and class.

God, I fucking love her.

I'm walking up the path toward headquarters to meet with David, but when he comes rushing out of the building, I can see by the look on his face that something is wrong.

Bloody hell, what now?

"What's going on?" I ask.

"I'm sorry, sir, but I can't accompany you today. Alice is bleeding, and I need to take her to the hospital. Nick will go with you."

"Of course," I reply. "Go now, and keep me informed. She's going to be okay, David."

"I hope so, sir. She lost a baby earlier this summer, and I don't want to go through that again."

"Go get her looked over," I say, clapping the other man on the shoulder. "And take a deep breath. She's healthy and young. She's going to be fine."

"Sir." He nods. "Thank you."

Just as he hurries away, Nick walks out to join me. Nick is Nina's detail, but they must have made other arrangements for today.

"I hope you enjoy clearing and wiping down tables," I say.

"It's one of my favorite ways to spend the day, Your Highness."

I laugh as we climb the hill to the car. "I like you, Nick."

It's been another busy day at Drips & Sips. Watching Aspen work has fast become one of my favorite pastimes. The way she moves quickly around the café, smiling and checking in with her customers, so full of energy and joy, makes me smile.

She clearly loves what she does.

I'm going to do everything in my power to ensure that we're here in Cunningham Falls more often than not so she can continue working here. I can work from anywhere with video calls and WiFi. We will have to make appearances, but those will be scheduled in advance.

I'm convinced that we can make our schedules work, basing out of both Montana and London. It'll just require some work and compromise, but doesn't every marriage?

"It looks like the last customers just left, Aspen," Nick says as he places a tray of dirty dishes on the counter.

"Excellent, go ahead and flip the lock," Aspen replies.

Nick does as she asks, and Aspen sighs in relief.

"Are you okay?" I ask her.

"I'm exhausted," she says, rubbing her eyes. "It's been a hell of a week. But I interviewed two candidates for the manager position today, and I think I found the right person for the job."

"You didn't offer it to Gretchen?"

Aspen bites her lip and shrugs a shoulder. "I

mentioned it to her, but I suspect that she'll stay when she goes back to Portland. And, frankly, I can't blame her. It'll be a fresh start for her."

I walk behind the counter and pull Aspen to me, enjoying the way she fits against me. This woman was made for me.

"I'm so sorry that you came home to such a mess."

"It could always be worse," she says but rests her forehead against my chest. "But thank you. This helps. *You* help more than you realize. I'm grateful that I have you to lean on. I'm a strong person, but—"

"But sometimes even strong people need someone to lean on," I finish for her and tuck a stray piece of red hair behind her ear. "Indeed. With Gretchen taken care of, and things calming down, perhaps we need a quiet evening tonight at the boathouse. Just the two of us. We'll sit out and watch the lake, and just *be*."

"That might be the best offer you've ever made me. Aside from the whole marriage thing."

"Your sassiness is coming back, darling."

"I must be feeling better. Speaking of, have you heard from David?"

"Yes. Alice is doing well. She hasn't lost the baby, thank goodness."

"That is good news."

I nod in agreement, just as there's a knock on the door.

"There's a man at the door," Nick says. "Do you want me to ask him what he wants?"

"Sure," Aspen says, still cuddled up to me.

We both turn in surprise as someone barges in, yelling.

"Where the fuck is she? TELL ME WHERE SHE IS!" Miles is a maniac, waving a gun around, his eyes bulging in rage.

"Miles?" Aspen scowls at the man, just as Nick advances on him. Before he can reach him, Miles turns and fires the pistol, hitting Nick in the shoulder, then he swings back to us.

I shield Aspen with my body.

"Miles, calm down," I say with a low voice, but I can see right away that there is no reasoning with this man.

And Nick is bleeding on the floor.

"Fuck you," he sputters. "I told that cunt if she tried to leave me, I'd fucking kill her and everyone she loves, and this bitch is the first on my list. You're the whore who kept telling her to leave me. That I'm a piece of shit."

Aspen's hands fist in my shirt, but her voice is steady.

"You're sick," she says. "Miles, you need help."

"I don't need shit!" He fires another shot, but thankfully he's aiming for the ceiling. I can hear sirens, grateful that someone called the police. "Now, tell me where that bitch is. She has it coming, in spades, for what she did to me."

"You beat her!" Aspen yells.

"She's fucking *mine*!" he yells back. "I can do as I

please with her. Now, tell me where she is or I'll kill you both."

"Miles—"

He shoots again. This time, he hits me, sending me back into Aspen. We crash to the floor just as the door bursts open, and there's yelling and more gunfire.

Blood everywhere.

On me.

From Aspen's head.

"Oh Jesus, no." I take her face in my hands. "Baby, wake up. Aspen. Talk to me, Aspen."

"Sir, we'll take it from here."

"He shot. I don't know what he hit, there's so much blood."

"He hit you, sir." I look down at the blood coming from my arm and then at the man standing over me. I recognize him. Why can't I think of his name? "Let's get this all cleaned up. Let me get to her so I can help her."

I nod and sit back as more paramedics, police officers, and firefighters file in, getting to all three of us, assessing the scene.

I look through the glass case and see Miles lying dead on the floor, a pool of blood around him.

"She has a pulse."

"Thank fuck." Someone wraps my arm, but I don't give a shit. I can't take my eyes off of the woman I love. A man—Sam?—presses a white cloth to her head while someone else takes her blood pressure.

"How's Nick?" I call out.

"I'm alive, sir," he calls back. "The perp is dead."

"Good."

"We're taking you all to the hospital. Now." Sam's face is grim as he looks down at me. "She's not coming to. That wound on the head is bad, Callum. Let's go."

∽

"If you don't let me go to her now, I'll have you fired," I growl at the nurse.

"I've been threatened with far scarier things than you," she says as she loads a syringe with something. "You need this shot, sir."

"Then give it to me and let me go."

"The doctor has to approve it."

"For fuck's sake," I mutter and push my uninjured hand through my hair. The bullet grazed my arm, leaving behind plenty of blood, but the wound will heal quickly. I got much worse when I was in the British Army years ago.

I'm mostly annoyed that they won't let me see Aspen.

"Just tell me if she's okay."

"I'm with you," she reminds me. "So, I'm not sure what's going on with her. But as soon as I'm finished with you, and the doctor approves it, you can go see her. Now, calm down, and this will go more smoothly."

"I almost lost her," I mutter. "Jesus, I just found her, and I almost lost her."

"I haven't heard anyone call a code," she says kindly. "Which tells me no one has died. Let them work on her, and me on you, and then we'll get you all healed up."

I nod, slightly appeased. Nothing is as important to me right now as making sure Aspen is safe and whole.

CHAPTER 17

~ASPEN~

It's bright in here.

I squint as I look around.

"Am I in the hospital?"

A man smiles down at me. "You're awake. Yes, you're in the emergency room. You have quite a concussion. You've been in and out since you arrived about an hour ago. I'm Doctor Hamilton."

"My head is killing me."

"I'm sure it is. We started some Tylenol. Because you weren't lucid, and we couldn't ask questions, we had to do a lab panel before giving you any medicine. How far along are you?"

I frown. "Far along from what?"

He looks up from his computer. "In your pregnancy."

"You have the wrong patient. I'm not pregnant."

"According to your labs, you are. I take it you didn't know. Given that, you're probably not too far along."

I close my eyes against the incessant pounding behind my forehead. "I'm not pregnant."

"I can show you the lab results," Dr. Hamilton offers. "You're definitely expecting. Congratulations."

I shake my head, but that only makes me nauseous, so I stop.

"You have one whopper of a concussion, Aspen. You'll need to take it easy for a few days, and you'll need constant monitoring."

"Where's Callum?" Everything from the café comes rushing back to me. "Oh my God, where's Callum? Is he okay?"

"He's two doors down. He's going to be just fine," the doctor assures me. "It was just a minor wound on his arm. You're the more injured of the two of you."

I sit back in relief. Oh, God. I almost lost him.

"And Nick?"

"I can't give you too much information on Nick because you're not family, but I can say he's going to be okay."

"Thank you." I move to stand up, but the room spins, and I fall back onto the bed.

"Where do you think you're going?" Dr. Hamilton asks.

"To Callum. I need him."

"Well, give me a few minutes to finish up here, and

you can see him. Both of you are impatient and stubborn, do you know that?"

"Yeah." I grin, despite the horrible headache. "It's one of our best traits."

He goes over my instructions for what I need to do for the next few days and suggests that I follow up with my primary physician as soon as possible.

"If I promise I'll go to the doctor *today*, will you let me see Callum?"

He sighs. "I'll let him come over in a few minutes, after I check him out one more time. Just relax, okay? You've undergone trauma, Aspen. Don't make me admit you overnight."

"I'll be a good girl," I assure him.

I'm pregnant.

Oh, God. Just the thought of that makes me sick to my stomach. I never thought I'd have more children. I didn't want them. Of course, I didn't plan to get married again, but here we are.

"Aspen?" Callum rushes into the room and over to me. "Darling, are you okay?"

"I'm pregnant," I blurt. "There's no other way to say it, and I can't sugarcoat it. I'm going to have a baby, and I'm so sorry because I know we were super careful. We *always* used condoms. I should have gone on the pill."

Callum's scared face transforms into an expression of pure joy.

"This is wonderful news! It may be earlier than I

would have planned, but having children with you is absolutely something I want."

"No." I reach for his hand, begging him to understand. "It's not good news, Callum. I don't want more children. I can't be a mother again."

"What are you saying?"

"I'm saying that this isn't what I want. At all. I had a child, and I lost her. The ache that lives inside of me from that loss is constant. It never goes away, Callum. And I can't fill it with another child. I can't replace her and just forget her as if she never existed at all. That isn't fair to her *or* to me, and I refuse to do it."

"Love." Callum climbs up on the bed with me and holds me close. "You're not replacing Emma. That's impossible. Your daughter will always be a part of your heart and soul, and nothing will ever change that."

"I can't do it again."

He tips up my chin so he can look me in the eyes.

"You were a wonderful mother, and what happened to Emma wasn't your fault. Do you understand that?"

"My mind understands," I reply slowly. "But in my heart, I always believed that if I'd been with them that day, I could have done something to save her."

"Or you would have died with them, and I wouldn't have you with me now."

I blink at the thought. "I never considered that."

"It wasn't your fault. It was a horrible accident, and I'm so sorry it happened. If I could change it for you, I would, even if that meant I lost you because you'd still have your husband. I would take the pain away in a heartbeat.

"Having our child doesn't erase your past, Aspen. It just means that we're moving forward. And Emma would want that for you."

"Emma loved babies," I whisper. "Do you think that Emma held this little one before sending him down to us?"

"I guarantee it," he replies. "And what a lovely thought that is, sweetheart."

"Yeah." I sniff, letting my tears fall. Tears of grief because my sweet daughter won't be here to meet her new sibling. And tears of joy because I have the chance to love another little someone the way I did my sweet Emma. "I didn't plan this."

"Clearly," he says with a chuckle. "But we can move up the wedding."

"No." I shake my head again, adamant about this. "I will not get married again because I'm pregnant, Callum. I did that before, and I won't do it again. As it is, people will talk and say that you're marrying me because you have to. I'm not going to add fuel to that fire."

"I do have to," he replies easily. "Being without you isn't an option for me."

"You know what I mean." But I place a kiss on his mouth. "And thank you for that."

"I'll marry you whenever you want. Tomorrow or next year, I don't care as long as you're my wife."

"I want to have the baby and then have a wedding here in Cunningham Falls next autumn. If we got married right away, and I have a baby in seven months, it'll be said that it was a shotgun wedding."

"Charming."

"And it's not."

"Of course, not. I proposed to you before I knew you were pregnant."

"No one knows that."

"Fuck them," he says. "Like we said before, it doesn't matter what the media says as long as you and I are on the same page. But I meant what I said. I'll marry you anytime at all, as long as you marry me."

"You can't get rid of me," I say. "And I'm sorry that I said I didn't want the baby. I do. I just have a lot of emotions running through me right now."

"I know." He kisses my forehead gently. "Seeing you lying there today, lifeless and bleeding, was something I never want to go through again. If I lost you—"

"No more loss," I insist and kiss him. "For either of us. We've had our share, and now I'm ready to move forward with you and this baby, as a family, and enjoy our wonderful life."

"Princess Aspen," he murmurs. "It has a nice ring to it."

"Mrs. Wakefield sounds even better."

"You're the only woman I've ever met who's averse to taking on a royal title."

"I'm not averse to it. But *princess* implies I belong to

the commonwealth. And *Mrs.* implies that I belong to you. And that's the most important thing, first and foremost. The rest is gravy."

"I knew it. The minute I saw you, I knew you'd change my life."

"Me, too." His eyes darken at my admission. "And I'm finally ready for you."

EPILOGUE

~ASPEN~

One Year Later

"I feel like I've been waiting a long time for this."

I smile at the king as he takes my hand and tucks it into the crook of his arm.

"Thank you for agreeing to let us have a small Montana wedding," I say. "I know that you and the people expect something big and fancy in London, but this suits Callum and me so much better."

Callum's father surveys the scene before us. We're outside, next to the lake with bouquets of wildflowers and sunflowers everywhere. My dress is white and simple. Perfect for an outdoor wedding in Cunningham Falls.

"It's a beautiful day," he replies with a nod. "And you're right, it suits you. We'll have something splashy in London later."

"He's handsome, isn't he?" I ask, staring down the aisle at Callum, who's currently holding our three-month-old son, Patrick.

"He looks just like his father," the king replies with a wink. "How could he go wrong?"

"How indeed?" I laugh and reach up to kiss his cheek. "Thank you for walking me down the aisle."

"It's an honor and my pleasure," he replies. "After all of the challenges you've been through, you deserve this happiness. I feel lucky to be able to witness it, and that my son is the one you chose to share it with."

"Don't make me cry today. I'm wearing makeup."

He chuckles. "Shall we get you married, then?"

"Absolutely. Patrick might get fussy, so let's get a move on."

"Why my son chose to have an infant as his best man, I have no idea."

"Callum's a proud father," I reply as we start to walk down the aisle, and everyone stands to watch.

Within seconds, we reach the love of my life, who passes our son to his father. The king nuzzles the baby, kisses his cheek, and then turns to sit with his wife, who's already dabbing at tears under her eyes.

"You're stunning," Callum whispers.

"You're charming," I reply as the ceremony begins. We speak of love, commitment, fidelity, and respect.

And when it's over, I'm Callum's wife.

He kisses me deeply, in front of everyone we care about the most. As he pulls away, an eagle soars above, calling out to us.

"She's here," Callum murmurs.

"And she always will be," I reply. "Now, let's celebrate."

NEWSLETTER SIGN UP

I hope you enjoyed reading this story as much as I enjoyed writing it! For upcoming book news, be sure to join my newsletter! I promise I will only send you news-filled mail, and none of the spam. You can sign up here:

https://mailchi.mp/kristenproby.com/newsletter-sign-up

ALSO BY KRISTEN PROBY:

Other Books by Kristen Proby

The With Me In Seattle Series

Come Away With Me
Under The Mistletoe With Me
Fight With Me
Play With Me
Rock With Me
Safe With Me
Tied With Me
Breathe With Me
Forever With Me
Stay With Me
Indulge With Me
Love With Me

ALSO BY KRISTEN PROBY:

Dance With Me
Dream With Me

Coming in 2020:
You Belong With Me
Imagine With Me
Shine With Me

Check out the full series here: https://www.kristenprobyauthor.com/with-me-in-seattle

The Big Sky Universe

Love Under the Big Sky
Loving Cara
Seducing Lauren
Falling for Jillian
Saving Grace

The Big Sky
Charming Hannah
Kissing Jenna
Waiting for Willa
Soaring With Fallon

Big Sky Royal
Enchanting Sebastian
Enticing Liam

ALSO BY KRISTEN PROBY:

Coming in 2020:
Taunting Callum

Check out the full Big Sky universe here: https://www.kristenprobyauthor.com/under-the-big-sky

Bayou Magic

Shadows

Coming in 2020:
Spells

Check out the full series here: https://www.kristenprobyauthor.com/bayou-magic

The Romancing Manhattan Series

All the Way
All it Takes

Coming in 2020
After All

Check out the full series here: https://www.kristenprobyauthor.com/romancing-manhattan

The Boudreaux Series

ALSO BY KRISTEN PROBY:

Easy Love
Easy Charm
Easy Melody
Easy Kisses
Easy Magic
Easy Fortune
Easy Nights

Check out the full series here: https://www.kristenprobyauthor.com/boudreaux

The Fusion Series

Listen to Me
Close to You
Blush for Me
The Beauty of Us
Savor You

Check out the full series here: https://www.kristenprobyauthor.com/fusion

From 1001 Dark Nights

Easy With You
Easy For Keeps
No Reservations
Tempting Brooke
Wonder With Me

ALSO BY KRISTEN PROBY:

Coming in 2020:
Shine With Me

Kristen Proby's Crossover Collection

Soaring with Fallon, A Big Sky Novel

Wicked Force: A Wicked Horse Vegas/Big Sky Novella
By Sawyer Bennett

All Stars Fall: A Seaside Pictures/Big Sky Novella
By Rachel Van Dyken

Hold On: A Play On/Big Sky Novella
By Samantha Young

Worth Fighting For: A Warrior Fight Club/Big Sky Novella
By Laura Kaye

Crazy Imperfect Love: A Dirty Dicks/Big Sky Novella
By K.L. Grayson

Nothing Without You: A Forever Yours/Big Sky Novella
By Monica Murphy

Check out the entire Crossover Collection here:

ALSO BY KRISTEN PROBY:

https://www.kristenprobyauthor.com/kristen-proby-crossover-collection

ABOUT THE AUTHOR

Kristen Proby has published close to fifty titles, many of which have hit the USA Today, New York Times and Wall Street Journal Bestsellers lists. She continues to self publish, best known for her With Me In Seattle and Boudreaux series, and is also proud to work with William Morrow, a division of HarperCollins, with the Fusion and Romancing Manhattan Series.

Kristen and her husband, John, make their home in her hometown of Whitefish, Montana with their two cats and dog.

- facebook.com/booksbykristenproby
- instagram.com/kristenproby
- bookbub.com/profile/kristen-proby
- goodreads.com/kristenproby

CPSIA information can be obtained
at www.ICGtesting.com
Printed in the USA
FSHW021627140820
72980FS